GOOD DOG, BAD COP

ALSO BY DAVID ROSENFELT

K TEAM NOVELS

Citizen K-9

Animal Instinct

The K Team

ANDY CARPENTER NOVELS

Santa's Little Yelpers

Holy Chow

Best in Snow

Dog Eat Dog

Silent Bite

Muzzled

Dachshund Through the Snow

Bark of Night

Deck the Hounds

Rescued

Collared

The Twelve Dogs of Christmas

Outfoxed

Who Let the Dog Out?

Hounded

Unleashed

Leader of the Pack

One Dog Night

Dog Tags

New Tricks

Play Dead

Dead Center

Sudden Death

Bury the Lead

First Degree

Open and Shut

THRILLERS

Black and Blue

Fade to Black

Blackout

Without Warning

Airtight

Heart of a Killer

On Borrowed Time

Down to the Wire

Don't Tell a Soul

NONFICTION

Lessons from Tara: Life Advice from the World's Most Brilliant Dog

Dogtripping: 25 Rescues, 11 Volunteers, and 3 RVs on Our Canine Cross-Country Adventure

GOOD DOG, BAD COP

DAVID ROSENFELT

MINOTAUR
BOOKS
NEW YORK

First published in the United States by Minotaur Books, an imprint of St. Martin's Publishing Group

GOOD DOG, BAD COP. Copyright © 2023 by Tara Productions, Inc. All rights reserved. Printed in the United States of America. For information, address St. Martin's Publishing Group, 120 Broadway, New York, NY 10271.

www.minotaurbooks.com

Designed by Omar Chapa

Library of Congress Cataloging-in-Publication Data

Names: Rosenfelt, David, author.
Title: Good dog, bad cop / David Rosenfelt.
Description: First edition. | New York : Minotaur Books, 2023. |
    Series: K Team Novels ; 4
Identifiers: LCCN 2022051657 | ISBN 9781250828965 (hardcover) |
    ISBN 9781250828972 (ebook)
Classification: LCC PS3618.O838 G66 2023 | DDC 813/.6—dc23
LC record available at https://lccn.loc.gov/2022051657

Our books may be purchased in bulk for promotional, educational, or business use. Please contact your local bookseller or the Macmillan Corporate and Premium Sales Department at 1-800-221-7945, extension 5442, or by email at MacmillanSpecialMarkets@macmillan.com.

First Edition: 2023

10 9 8 7 6 5 4 3 2 1

GOOD DOG, BAD COP

IT HAD BEEN A WHILE SINCE DANNY AVERY WAS ON ANYTHING RESEMBLING a stakeout.

Of course, this could never be classified as a normal stakeout. No one else in the Paterson Police Department knew where he was or what he was doing; Avery was working this one independently.

At some point they would find out, but by then the operation would be over.

Of course, if it wasn't successful, they'd never hear about it. Because in that case he sure as hell would not be filing a report about it.

Fortunately, this action tonight was not going to last long—two hours at most. Then Avery would follow his subject, approach him when he was alone, and drop the hammer on him.

He was very much looking forward to that.

Avery was well positioned on the darkened street, far

enough away that he could not be seen, but absolutely in a place where he could not miss seeing the target when he appeared. Avery was pretty confident that no one had seen him, certainly not the people he was after.

He could hear their conversation through the planted wire, and it was going exactly as he hoped. He was recording it on his phone and would ultimately make good use of that audio.

But for the moment Avery would have to wait, anxiously, because this night would be the night it would all start to come together, one way or the other. It had taken a lot of time, and the next two hours would seem like no time at all by comparison.

Avery's reputation, and his future in the department, were on the line, and this would change the trajectory of both for the better.

Two hours.

Danny Avery never heard the noise or felt the impact. The back of his head exploded, sending blood and brain matter all across the dashboard and the front windshield, which shattered when the bullet reached it.

His assailant reached into the car, grabbed Avery's cell phone from the dash, and fled into the night, unseen.

THE IDEA OF PEOPLE GETTING AWAY WITH MURDER PISSES ME OFF, WHICH
is why the past two days have been so infuriating.

My name is Corey Douglas, and along with my partners
Laurie Collins and Marcus Clark, we call ourselves the K Team.
That name is in honor of the fourth member of our squad, Simon
Garfunkel, the German shepherd who retired from the Paterson
Police Department when I did.

Naming our group was Laurie's idea, and I reluctantly went
along. I pointed out that we are private investigators, not a
bowling team. But I gave in because there's no harm in a name,
so it just wasn't a big deal. I would certainly have drawn the
line at wearing uniforms if anyone had suggested it.

Even though we are private investigators, we've recently
been at least partially on the public payroll. That's because Pete
Stanton, the captain in charge of the Homicide Division of the
Paterson PD, has hired us to investigate cold cases.

Pete had explained that financial restrictions were preventing him from hiring new cops, but that a budget anomaly provided funds for hiring consultants. He figured if he didn't spend the money, he wouldn't get credit for being frugal. The bureaucrats would just take back the money.

So we are the chosen consultants . . . well-paid chosen consultants at that. I'm making three times what I made in my days on the force, overtime included. Best of all, I don't have to punch a clock, and nobody is looking over my shoulder.

Pete has given us general freedom to decide which cold cases we're interested in tackling, though he has to sign off on them. So for the last two days here at the station we've been going through the files he's provided, which have been among the most unpleasant days I can remember.

As an ex-cop, I am aware of the awful things that people can do to each other, and how often they do them. So going through these cases, which consist of one unsolved murder after another, does not shock or enlighten me.

But it does depress me, and it certainly angers me, since each case represents at least one person that has literally gotten away with murder. Unless the killers have been convicted of another crime and put away, they are living among us, going about their business after having deprived someone else of their very life.

The friends and family of those victims have never gotten any kind of closure, which must drive them crazy.

It sure bugs the hell out of me.

There are few of these cases that I wouldn't want to tackle; I'd like to systematically put every one of these assholes behind bars. But we have to do it one at a time, and the one I am most interested in is not even in the files Pete provided.

Laurie, Marcus, and I had discussed this when Pete first

talked to us about taking on the cold cases. We agreed that if any one of us had a deep personal interest in a case, then the others would defer and let that person choose.

I have such an interest, and since we're all in Pete's office about to tell him our choice, he's about to hear it. But he's not going to like it.

"Jimmy Dietrich and Susan Avery," I say.

The look on Pete's face is completely predictable; it's as if he's just taken a sip of a horseshit smoothie. "Don't go there."

"That's our pick. Or at least it's my pick, and my partners are willing to indulge me."

"We're good that way," Laurie says.

Pete shakes his head. "It wasn't even in the case files I gave you."

"We noticed that," I say. "Obviously an oversight by you. But the Jimmy Dietrich, Susan Avery case is still our choice."

Pete is getting frustrated. "As you may remember, the idea of this arrangement is for you to find out who committed crimes that are currently unsolved."

Laurie jumps in again. "This case fits that directive, Pete, especially the Susan Avery piece. There's no question that she was murdered, and no one has been officially identified as her killer."

"You know damn well why that is," he says. "If you were to get into this, the strong possibility is that you would not like what you find, if you find anything at all."

I nod. "Maybe. Or maybe not. We won't know until we know."

"So if that's the way it turns out, if you prove what happened, who will be better off for it?"

"We'll know the truth, Pete," I say. "That will have to be good enough."

Pete shakes his head. "I'm not convinced. Besides, the case is what . . . a year and a half old? It hasn't had time to turn cold. It's lukewarm."

"Have you had people working it lately?"

"You know I haven't."

"Then it's cold," I say.

He remains obviously unconvinced. "I'll have to think about it. What's your second choice?"

"We don't have a second choice, Pete," Laurie says.

I look at Laurie, and she nods her silent agreement at what she knows I'm going to say next.

"How about if we make it a two-for-one?" We knew how this conversation would go, so we held this out as a bargaining chip to close the deal.

"I'm listening." Pete also knows full well where this is going.

"We'll look into Danny Avery as well."

Pete smiles. "Now you're talking."

JUDGES AND JURIES ARE SUPPOSED TO BE COMPLETELY IMPARTIAL; THE system falls apart if they are not.

But while they are the last line of defense against bias, the entire process starts with, and depends on, the investigating detective. Detectives must have no predispositions whatsoever; they must rigidly follow the facts wherever they lead. If they don't, and they arrest the wrong person, they might put an innocent man away. And maybe just as bad, the real criminal will never be found and punished.

When it comes to finding out what happened to Jimmy Dietrich, Susan Avery, and Danny Avery, I am going to fail that test miserably. I will follow the evidence, but I will be biased every step of the way. Fortunately Laurie and Marcus will know that and will rein me in as best they can.

Right now I'm discussing this with Dani Kendall. We're at Patsy's, the best pizza place in both Paterson, New Jersey, and on planet Earth. Having grown up in Teaneck, Dani had never been to Patsy's until I took her when we started dating. Now she can't get enough of it, one of many reasons I am crazy about her.

"So you're biased . . . so what?" she says, after I explain the situation to her. "That just makes you human."

"Cops aren't supposed to be biased; it's not part of the job description. And they definitely aren't supposed to be human."

"Bullshit. Everybody is biased. The trick is to overcome it and be fair and accurate. You've been doing that your whole life . . . when you were officially a cop, and ever since. I don't think you could stop if you tried."

"How did you turn into such a know-it-all?"

"By knowing everything. Actually, I don't know everything; I couldn't tune a carburetor if you gave me two years and a YouTube video. But I do know you. You'll follow the facts; it's what you do."

I chew on some pizza while thinking about what she's just said. Pizza is definitely good thinking food. "I do not believe Jimmy killed anyone, including himself."

"Then prove it. Or find out you were wrong. Either one is better than not knowing."

"In theory that's correct. But in real life, not knowing would be preferable to finding out that Jimmy committed a murder-suicide. I would have troubling handling that."

She points to the last piece of pizza on the tray. "You going to eat that?" As she says it, she reaches for the piece and takes a bite out of it.

"Apparently not. I was going to suggest we share it."

She smiles, finishes chewing. "You hesitated. You can't hesitate in the pizza business."

I take a few moments to reflect on the state of my relationship with Dani. I have only started to do self-reflection since meeting her; prior to that, the last time I attempted it was when I was in high school and tried to figure out why Rita Barone wouldn't go to the prom with me. I couldn't come up with anything.

When I invited her, she had said, "Not on a bet, Corey," which was fairly disconcerting. It's actually still disconcerting, which is why I haven't reflected on it since.

But my current situation is unlike anything I have ever before experienced. Until Dani, most of my relationships lasted about an hour and a half, give or take forty-five minutes. I liked it that way, and I had no intention of changing.

But Dani tricked me by being funny, smart, beautiful, and independent. It was diabolical, and it has left me thinking about the M-word.

It's a measure of my maturity in relationships that even in my own mind I call it the M-word. I know that two adults who are in love and want to spend the rest of their lives together often naturally decide to M, but I'm not yet at the point where I can say the entire word.

I wish I had never started this reflection stuff because it's made me realize that Dani might not want to M me if I asked. I mean, she has never brought it up, not once. Never even hinted at it. Is that normal for a woman who wants to get M . . . ed? I think not.

I guess I could ask Laurie what she thinks, since she and Dani have become good friends, but that doesn't seem mature. It would feel like I was asking her to pass Dani a note in homeroom. I've talked about it with Simon Garfunkel, but he's absolutely no help. He didn't even wag his tail when I brought it up.

Another reason I don't want to talk about it with Laurie is because then it would be out there, an open subject that would have to be dealt with one way or the other. As long as the idea resides solely in my warped brain, it feels like I preserve my options.

But what if I don't have any options? What if Dani just isn't interested in M? I don't handle rejection well, which is why I almost never put myself in a position to get rejected. As a cop I often put myself in a position to get killed, but emotional rejection? Never.

I'm not about to start now, so that's it . . . end of discussion, end of reflection. M is not for me.

"You've gotten suddenly quiet," Dani says.

"I'm just bitter that you took the last piece of pizza." No way I'm going to tell her the truth; the M-word is not coming out of my mouth.

It won't even be in my mind for long anyway. There is a case to focus on, and a mentor and friend to exonerate.

I've got a bias to justify.

"PETE KNEW WE'D TAKE BOTH CASES," I SAY. "HE PLAYED US WHILE WE were playing him."

Laurie nods. "And we all got what we want. A win-win."

Laurie, Marcus, and I are meeting to discuss how we are going to tackle our assignment. We do this every time we start a case, though whatever strategy we come up with quickly gets changed as soon as we begin.

Investigations are like that. It reminds me of Mike Tyson's comment that everyone he fought came into the ring with a plan that lasted until they got punched in the mouth.

We're at Laurie's house, which has become our de facto office. It's not that we're too cheap to rent space, though not having to is a definite plus. It's more that in many cases we're working for Laurie's husband, Andy Carpenter, who is a defense attorney. And even though he maintains an office downtown, he generally likes to work out of his house, where his wife, son, and dogs reside.

Since Andy tries his best to avoid taking on clients, he's usually around the house. Laurie frequently takes advantage of this by sending him out to get us pizza, sandwiches, and other sustenance, and he grumbles but ultimately does it. The next time we reimburse him will be the first.

Another benefit of being here is that the fourth member of our team, Simon Garfunkel, likes Andy and Laurie's three dogs, especially their golden retriever, Tara. There is also no shortage of biscuits here, and Simon is definitely partial to biscuits.

Since we were both cops in the Paterson Police Department, Laurie and I are familiar with the murders of Danny Avery, Susan Avery, and Jimmy Dietrich. I think of Jimmy's death as a murder because I do not think he could have committed suicide.

That's my bias and I'm sticking to it.

Marcus, not having been in the department, is not as aware of the details of the case as we are. We'll be getting copies of the murder books, so he'll learn all there is to know, but we want to bring him up to speed now.

"Danny Avery was a detective that I worked with briefly," Laurie says. "You may have heard of him; there was quite a bit of publicity when he shot and killed a suspect in a domestic violence incident. He took a lot of heat for it."

Marcus nods slightly; at least I think he's nodding, he could be dozing off. Talking and listening are not Marcus's favorite pastimes, which is deceptive, because he is one of the smartest people I know.

But he's at his best in situations that call for violence. Marcus is outstanding at it; if violence was on the SATs, Harvard would have been his safety school.

Laurie continues, "Avery was shot and killed, execution-style, while sitting in his car on Chamberlain Avenue. He was off duty, and to my knowledge it's unclear why he was there, and no suspect was ever identified. It was about four months after the domestic violence incident."

"Jimmy Dietrich wasn't the detective on the case," I say, "but the cops who did handle it got nowhere. I know it bothered Jimmy a lot; he knew Danny and his wife, Susan, very well. And to see a cop gunned down like that . . ."

A nod from Marcus; he's awake.

I continue, "Then Jimmy retired, and it didn't go well. He couldn't handle being away from the job, his marriage went south, and the word was he was drinking too much. He tried to come back to the department, but he was told it was against policy.

"Then one day they found Jimmy and Susan Avery dead on Jimmy's boat, floating in the ocean outside of Long Island Sound. She was shot at short range; he took the bullet in the head, point-blank. The coroner said she couldn't classify it with any certainty. It was either a double murder or a murder-suicide, but without any way to be sure, it was left open."

Laurie chimes in, "But most people thought it was murder-suicide, and the department was criticized for not deciding one way or the other. They were thought to be protecting their own, which might well be true."

"Or not," I say.

She nods, somewhat grudgingly. "Or not." Then, "So that's the basic setup; obviously we'll learn a lot more when we see the investigative reports. So where do we start?"

"Everywhere," I say. "We could be dealing with two entirely different cases; at this point there is no specific evidence linking Danny Avery's murder with the others. But they obviously could be connected, and I think they are. So we look at the whole package and see if there is a link."

Laurie nods. "And if not, we solve them separately."

"I'll take the lead on the Jimmy Dietrich–Susan Avery side. I know most of the players in Jimmy's life; they'll be more likely to open up to me."

Laurie doesn't look pleased with this; I know she thinks that my lack of objectivity could hamper us. But she finally nods her agreement. "Okay. But we all need to pay attention to the Danny Avery side. We have to operate under the assumption that it was not a random shooting by someone who hates cops, that Danny was targeted. Because if that's not the case, then we have no chance."

"Right," I say. "And if it was random, then it's totally separate from the other half of our case. Which is not the way I think this is going to go; I think one ultimately led to the others."

Laurie says, "We're supposed to have all the paper by this afternoon; Pete is sending it here. Once we go through it, if anything strikes anyone as particularly worth pursuing, then we meet again to talk about it."

Marcus nods and I say, "That's a wrap."

SIMON AND I ARE GOING FOR A RUN THIS MORNING.

As far as I can recall, this is his first time experiencing it. That's because he's nine, and it's been at least nine years since I've been on a run myself.

Not that I haven't done any running in that time; I certainly have. I've played basketball, tennis, and racquetball, and on more than one occasion I've sprinted after perpetrators to make an arrest.

But since I reached adulthood, I can't remember ever running when the sole purpose was the running itself; it's always seemed stupid and unproductive.

Since my retirement I've gained a few pounds, and I'm pretty sure Dani has noticed because she commented that I'm "porking up." She's subtle that way. So this run is a first step toward getting back in great shape.

I find running, when it's not part of a sports competition,

to be incredibly boring. Simon, apparently, has a different view. He's eager and into it, running ahead of me and looking back in disdain at my sluggish pace. Since he's on a leash, he's stuck with me, and he's clearly annoyed by it.

My plan is to run two miles, and I complete about 25 percent of my plan before I wrap it up. Simon's not happy about it, but since he relies on me for food and biscuits, he has to be careful how abusive he can be.

"We'll do it again tomorrow, big guy," I lie. I can't imagine that he believes me; Simon is a smart dog.

I shower, give Simon a chewie, and watch him settle in for a nap. He's been sleeping more and more lately, no doubt a sign of aging that I refuse to acknowledge. But even in retirement, he's still as good a police dog as there is anywhere.

I go outside and wait for Laurie to pick me up so we can check out one of the murder scenes together. She arrives at noon, right on time, and when the car pulls up, she rolls down the passenger window and says, "Get in the back."

I'm a trained detective, so I immediately realize that unless this is a remote-control car, someone else has joined us.

Sure enough, I'm right again. The driver of the car is Andy Carpenter, Laurie's husband. Andy and I have a somewhat complicated relationship. Years ago he attacked me in a cross-examination when I was a cop testifying for the prosecution. He made me look foolish, and I've never lost my bitterness about that.

On the other hand, he has since represented me when I was wrongly accused of murder and brilliantly managed to keep me from going to jail for the rest of my life. And he did the entire thing, including a lengthy trial, for free.

Maybe I should get over my bitterness.

"I thought it would just be the two of us," I say after we exchange hellos.

"Andy is going to buy lunch."

"On the other hand, three is the perfect number for checking out murder scenes."

We head down to Chamberlain Avenue, which has a combination of private homes and businesses, including an excellent Italian restaurant called Marcella's. But the location we're heading for is pretty far up the street from it.

We pull up and park at an address in front of a private home. Laurie says, "This is exactly where Danny Avery was when he was shot. He was sitting in his car at eight forty-five at night."

"But no one knows why he was here," I say.

"Do we know how long he was parked here before he got shot?" Andy asks.

"Around thirty-five minutes; the owner of the house saw him pull up," Laurie says. "She didn't realize that he stayed in the car, so she didn't think anything of it. She thought maybe the parking lot that the restaurant uses was overcrowded, and he was going to dinner."

I turn and look at the parking lot, which right now only has about five cars in it. It's still early for the lunchtime crowd. The lot is quite a bit closer to where we are than the restaurant, which is much farther down the street.

"Was the assailant on foot?" Andy asks.

Laurie responds. "No, apparently not. A car was seen leaving the scene, going that way, past the restaurant. A bystander got the license plate, but it was stolen."

"This was no random shooting," I say. "Avery was in street clothes, sitting in a civilian vehicle, so it wasn't some asshole out cop-hunting. And it's quiet and dark here; at night the odds that someone would be driving along and even notice that he was in the car are small. The shooter had to have followed Avery here and waited for the right moment, then took him out."

Neither Andy nor Laurie say anything, which tells me that they agree, because neither is ever shy about disagreeing.

Finally Andy asks, "Did the police check who was in the restaurant that night? Avery could have been following them, and waiting for them to leave."

"They discounted it. We can't see the front of the restaurant from here. Avery would have gotten closer to make sure he saw the person leaving. There were probably open spots closer, but still far enough for him to not be detected."

"Okay, let's have lunch," Andy says. "I recommend Marcella's. We can walk to it, and they have great pasta."

We head down to the restaurant, and the lack of a reservation does not stop us from being seated. Andy points to a table near the front, by the window. "Is that table available?"

The maître d' nods and leads us to that table. They bring over the menus, and Laurie and I look at them, while Andy stares out the window.

"We can't see our car from here," he says. "Avery couldn't have seen the front of the restaurant, nor could anyone in the restaurant have seen him."

"We've already established that," Laurie says.

Andy nods. "I know. But I still think that's why Avery was here. He was on a stakeout, waiting for someone to come out. It's the logical explanation."

"How do you figure?" I ask. Andy can be obnoxious, but he's smart. He could well be getting at something important.

"He was watching the parking lot, which he could definitely see from his car. Whoever he was following must have parked there, so Avery was smart enough to know he didn't have to be close to the front of the restaurant, where he might be seen. He just had to watch the parking lot, to see when the target returned to his car."

I'm mentally trying to punch holes in the theory and not coming up with anything. Laurie's silence tells me she's having the same reaction. "Not bad," I say. "Glad you came along."

"Do I still have to pay for lunch?"

"Yes," Laurie and I say in unison.

COMPUTERS ARE THE BEST THING TO HAPPEN TO DETECTIVES SINCE humans grew fingerprints.

I know some old-school people may bemoan the day our society became computerized; they're the same people who long for the days of quill pens and carbon paper. But I never met a cop who felt that way.

Everything about cataloging evidence is enhanced 1,000,000 percent by technology. It's the reason that DNA, fingerprints, and even faces can be checked against nationwide databases in seconds. It is remarkable how many cases have been solved by this process. Even cops like me who know nothing about technology rely on it.

Another among the many positives that computers provide for cops is that there are easily accessible records of almost everything. Our situation right now is a perfect example of what I'm talking about.

The cops never checked to learn who was dining at Marcella's the night that Danny Avery was killed. I understand that to a degree: they knew that Avery was far enough down the street that he could not see the front of the restaurant, so there was no reason to think he was following anyone inside.

Maybe they were right. Maybe Andy's point about the parking lot, while logical, is incorrect. Maybe Avery was parked where he was for another reason altogether, one having nothing to do with the restaurant.

But the cops never thought about the parking lot, so they never considered the restaurant patrons to be important. In a precomputer world, we could never go back and reconstruct who was there; the handwritten reservation sheet would have been discarded long ago.

But the system is computerized, and I can't imagine any reason for the restaurant to have discarded those records. They don't fill filing cabinets to overflowing; they don't become yellowed with age.

Even if they have deleted them, we might be able to go in through the back door, by getting their credit card logs for that night. It would be more complicated, but we have a way to deal with that.

Sam Willis is our secret weapon in this area. Sam is Andy's accountant, but he is also an expert computer hacker who possesses the astonishing ability to get into any computer system, anywhere. If we have to, we can get Sam to find out anything in the restaurant's system. It's not necessarily legal, but over time I've dealt with that moral issue.

I still don't see myself as an end-justifies-the-means guy, but I've learned to make exceptions.

It won't be long until we know what we'll need to handle this situation. Since we're not cops, we can't speak with the authority of the police department any longer. Pete Stanton has sent an officer to the restaurant to request the records that we need, and Sam Willis has gone along to deal with any technological issues or questions that might arise.

Sometimes business owners are reluctant to turn over records, no matter who is making the request and how unimportant they are to the operation of the business. A distrust for authority has become pretty widespread these days, and we'll soon be learning whether the owner of Marcella's shares that attitude.

We could always get a subpoena, but that is somewhat time-consuming and can be challenged. If the owner is not forthcoming, we might have to save time by putting Sam's magic to work.

Sam calls me with a report after going to the restaurant, and I conference Laurie into the call. Dani taught me how to do conferencing, but it remains a miracle that I'm able to manage it.

Marcus is not included; he has made it clear he doesn't want to be a part of calls like this. He prefers the action side of things. He likes to get assignments to carry out, and his success rate in doing so is 100 percent. Marcus is the type of person for whom the term *ruthless efficiency* was coined.

"Okay," Sam says, "the restaurant says they still have the reservation records in their computer, and they are going to find them and give them to the cops, who will turn them over to us. That's the good news."

"What's the bad?" Laurie asks.

"Well, all that will show is who made the reservation, and how many people were in the party. It won't show who else was there."

"Understood," I say.

"So I asked if they had the credit card records. Sometimes

the person who made the reservation would have paid, but sometimes not. It would increase our knowledge of who was there."

"But they don't have them?"

"I think they do, but it's complicated and they don't want to be bothered, so they said they discarded them. They might also not want to give out sensitive information, thinking it could come back to haunt them if the customers find out and get pissed off."

"So we should try for a subpoena," Laurie says.

"Up to you," Sam says. "But I'm sure I could get in there and find it. Unless it really has been deleted. And if not, I could go in through a different door."

We've been in this situation a bunch of times before. Having Sam get it is not strictly legal; in fact it's not legal at all. But it's much faster, and we can eventually get the information anyway through a subpoena. That's how I often rationalize doing it Sam's way.

Laurie says, "Go for it, Sam."

I AM TECHNOLOGICALLY INCOMPETENT, AND I'M FINE WITH THAT.

I also can't do electrical wiring or treat illnesses or fly a plane. But as long as there are people who can do those things, people that I have access to, then I'm content with my ignorance. That's how I feel about computers and technology.

But if there is one technological concept I can happily accept, and even embrace, it's rebooting. It's like a miracle . . . something doesn't work, so you turn it off, then turn it back on, and it works!

I no longer have to do the things I used to do when something failed. No more swearing at it or kicking it or calling a repairman or throwing it out. Actually, kicking it twice is what I initially assumed rebooting meant.

I googled it but could not find the name of the person who invented rebooting, but he or she is an uncredited genius. Having said that, the greatest achievement of all will come from the person who is able to apply rebooting to other areas of life.

Just imagine the applications it would have.

What if I could have rebooted striking out in extra innings against Lyndhurst in the championship game? How much would I have loved to reboot my SAT performance? Or my first week on the force when I stopped the mayor for speeding?

And think of the sexual implications that rebooting could have.

Right now, if I were given the gift of retroactive rebooting, I would apply it to my relationship with Jimmy Dietrich . . . specifically the last two months of his life. He was my friend, like a father to me. But he was in trouble, and I wasn't there for him.

I tried, but not nearly hard enough. I called him a bunch of times, if three or four constitutes a bunch. Jimmy was not interested in talking, claiming that he was busy and my concern was unwarranted. I wouldn't say he was cold; he just sounded uninterested and maybe preoccupied.

Each time he ended the conversation with a half-hearted statement about getting together "when we have time." I should have pressed him more; I had heard the rumors that he was drinking and depressed, and I shouldn't have let him off the hook. I took the easy way out.

Part of the problem, if I want to rationalize and excuse myself, which I do, is that there was no one else to talk to. I didn't feel comfortable calling his soon-to-be-ex-wife, Caroline. Although I had a good relationship with her over the years, I was clearly Jimmy's friend, and I didn't think calling her about Jimmy's welfare would be well received by either of them.

But bottom line is that I blew it, and I've been "booting" and "rebooting" myself for it ever since.

While it's obviously way too late to change Jimmy's fate, I've just called Caroline to talk, and she was completely receptive. I'm glad about that, but it makes me feel even dumber for not calling her back when I could have made a difference.

Caroline invited me to come over right away, which is why I am headed to Leonia now. She didn't ask me what I wanted; she just seemed eager to connect. I'm afraid she'll be annoyed and disappointed when she finds out it's not a social call, but I've annoyed and disappointed a lot of women before.

It would take forever to reboot them all.

She asked me to bring Simon; like everyone else, she remembers and loves him. She lives on a quiet street, a modest home with a small but perfectly manicured lawn and garden. I park in front, walk up the three steps, and ring the bell. I'm surprised when a man comes to the door.

"Detective Douglas?"

When he says that, I realize that Caroline might not realize that I retired from the force. "Yes."

"Come in. Caroline is expecting you. And this must be Simon."

"Yes, it certainly must."

"I've heard a great deal about you both." Then, "Caroline! Detective Douglas is here."

Caroline comes into the room, a big smile on her face, and she gives me a warm hug in greeting. "Corey, it has been way too long," she says, then gets down on one knee to give Simon a proper hug as well.

She introduces the guy as her fiancé, Gary; her planning to be remarried hits home how long I've been out of the Caroline loop. Caroline invites me into the den to have coffee, and Gary discreetly disappears.

We sit down in the den, and she brings out coffee and blueberry muffins. They're homemade, and they trigger a pleasant memory of the days when she used to serve them to Jimmy and me while we played gin in this house.

Jimmy and I always played for money, but we kept a running total; no one ever actually paid. I think when he died, I was up almost two dollars. I think I'll write it off.

Once we're settled in, she says, "So how are things in the department?"

"I'm sure they're fine, but I retired a while back. I took my pension, they gave Simon a gold biscuit, and neither of us has looked back."

"That's wonderful. I'm happy to hear it. One less person to worry about." She points to Simon. "Make that two less to worry about."

I smile. "Jimmy knew you always worried about him."

She nods, remembering. "Every time he left the house to go to work, for as long as he was on the job. After that I still worried about him, but for a different reason." Then, "So this is a social call? I was afraid it was about Jimmy's death."

"Well, not exactly a social call, though I am very happy to see you. I'm a private investigator now, and Pete Stanton has hired us to look into both Jimmy's murder and the Avery killings as well."

"You think Jimmy was murdered?" Her expression reveals her surprise. "My sense at the time was that everyone thought he committed suicide."

"I was going to ask you the same question."

"I do think he was murdered. And the more I think about it, the more I do. There is no way Jimmy would take his own life."

"But he was going through a rough time; that was obvious to everybody. I know you and Jimmy weren't together at the time of his death, but—"

She interrupts, "A very rough time. He just couldn't handle leaving the life. He actually tried to get back in, but they wouldn't let him. He understood that was the policy, but it still hurt him. It was as if outside the life he couldn't find an identity."

The life is what Jimmy and just about every other cop in the department calls being on the force. It always seemed arrogant to me, even though I also used the term. People of every occupation, from factory worker to advertising executive to physician, live their own version of "the life." On the force we were simply working a job, just like everybody else. We were living *a* life, not *the* life.

She continues, "So he started to drink and obsess over cases he never solved. And then he drank more and obsessed more, until I couldn't take it. I tried, Corey, I really tried. But he shut me and everyone else out."

"How much do you know about what he was doing in those weeks near the end?"

"Not a lot. He called sometimes, mostly to try and see if I had any interest in getting back together. And then we talked about the terms for what would have been our divorce. Those were very painful times."

"So you never got divorced?" I had heard that but it was never confirmed.

"No. It was on track to happen, but then Jimmy died. Divorce is a two-person operation. So I officially became a widow instead."

"How was he spending his time?"

"I honestly don't know, but my sense was he was finally getting his head on straight, or at least straighter. He seemed better the last weeks before he died, although I guess it could have been an act. He called a lot, came over a few times . . . he said he had stopped drinking; I don't know if that was true or not."

"Do you know what his relationship was with Susan Avery?"

"I don't, but I know they were connected in some way. She called him once when he was here visiting. Whatever she wanted, it made him leave right away to deal with it."

I should have brought Laurie along to ask the next question; she's about four thousand times more tactful than me. But I just need to go for it. "Could there have been anything between them?"

Caroline doesn't seem put off by the question at all. "I've asked myself that a lot. Bottom line, while it's certainly possible, I doubt it very much. He was too consumed by other things, and, to be unkind, way too self-absorbed at that time. But even if he was involved with her, he was entitled. We were getting the divorce."

"Did he know Danny Avery well?"

"Yes, he was a mentor to Danny. Not like with you; that was special. But I remember it bothered Jimmy terribly when Danny had that incident."

I remember the incident that she's referring to. Avery was well thought of in the department, on a fast promotion track. Then he was called to a domestic violence incident, which rapidly went south. He wound up shooting and killing the perpetrator.

He was deemed to have acted properly, but there was controversy in the press about whether he had to have used deadly force. Contributing to the backlash was that the deceased had no prior record, was well off financially, and was even something of a philanthropist.

Critics of police tried to make Avery a poster boy for the use of unnecessary and deadly force, although there was no real justification for that view. But all the publicity damaged Avery's career significantly; and after that it seemed his star was no longer on the rise internally.

She continues, "And then of course Jimmy was distraught when Danny was killed."

"Did he ever talk about that case?"

"Just to express his anger and grief over it. That's all I remember."

"I wish I could have helped Jimmy more. I feel like I let him down."

"He never felt that way, Corey. He loved you like a son. But I know what you're saying; in a way I have the same thoughts about it myself."

"You did what you could, Caroline."

"Thank you, but even though we were finished as a couple, I don't think I've ever gotten what people call closure. I always thought there would be more time, and then suddenly there wasn't. I've never even gone through his office; I keep saying I will, and then I don't."

I smile. "I'll tell you what. You stop beating yourself up, and I'll stop beating myself up. I suspect Jimmy wouldn't want us to."

"Okay, Corey. Let's try."

JUST BASED ON THE VOLUME OF INVESTIGATIVE RECORDS, THE POLICE clearly spent more time on the Danny Avery murder than the deaths of Susan Avery and Jimmy Dietrich.

It's not that they totally dropped the ball on the latter case; the investigation was significant in both time and manpower. But on some level they obviously believed that Jimmy committed a murder-suicide, and I think there was a subconscious reluctance to prove it.

When I get back to Laurie's house, she and Marcus are going through the large Danny Avery murder book. It's a painstaking task. Investigating the murder of a cop when there are no obvious leads is as difficult as it gets.

A smart investigator will go after motive and try to figure out who had a grudge against the victim and maybe wanted him dead. The problem is, when it comes to a cop, and especially a detective like Danny Avery, there is no shortage of such people.

Avery put a lot of people in prison, and criminals that go to prison tend to be pissed off. They are also often violent, and the combination could have resulted in a bullet to Danny Avery's head.

But we need to go through all the possibilities again, as if starting from scratch. That's not to say we won't pay attention to the many interviews and efforts that the detectives cataloged, but we have to think and hope that they missed something. Maybe our fresh eyes, and the fact that we're not working on twelve cases at once, can find something important.

One of the things that we will do, that we know for sure the cops did not do, is compare the list of potential suspects with the patron list we will get from the restaurant. In a perfect world we'll get a match, but I cannot remember the last time the world turned out to be perfect.

I pitch in to help go through everything, and Simon heads off to find Tara. A few minutes later Andy leaves to take their three dogs on a walk, and he asks if Simon can come along. Andy said that the last time he walked all four dogs, someone stopped in their car and asked for his card, thinking he was a professional dog walker.

I don't know what Andy said in reply, but I doubt it was polite and respectful.

The list of potential grudge holders against Danny Avery is long, though I'd bet a list of mine would be even longer. But this process is not quite as daunting for us as it was for the original investigators because they were able to eliminate some candidates.

For example, if the person was in jail when Danny Avery was killed, then he was certainly not the shooter. Of course, that's not to say he didn't hire the shooter.

Underlying all this is the knowledge that if the murder of Avery was random, then we are never going to get anywhere. It's way too late to pick up the trail if there was no motive that we can track.

Random shootings when there is no forensic evidence are close to impossible to solve. The only hope is a tip from someone who knows the shooter, but after all this time that is not about to happen.

We're going to simultaneously work the Susan Avery– Jimmy Dietrich case, but it makes sense that we pay extra attention at this point to Danny Avery. That's because his killing might have led to the later deaths; chronologically, there is no possibility that the reverse is true.

I'm going into this thinking that there's a decent possibility that all the murders are connected. Certainly Susan Avery's relationship to Danny links them. But if we are going to find that connective tissue, it's more likely to start with Danny Avery.

We divide the possible suspects into two groups. One group includes the people that the investigators eliminated as the potential perpetrator, for whatever reason. The other group includes those who could not be eliminated, but who weren't tied to the crime by existing evidence.

We will look into all the names in both groups, since some people may have been ruled out incorrectly. We will also hopefully create a third group, consisting of serious suspects that the police missed entirely the first time.

It's a slog, and after four hours, Laurie asks if we're hungry. Both Marcus and I answer yes.

She calls Andy in. "We're all hungry."

Andy nods. "I'll alert the media."

"How about bringing in some takeout?"

"What am I, DoorDash?"

Andy can be a tad caustic, but Laurie is undeterred. "No, if you were DoorDash, we'd have to pay for the food."

"God forbid," Andy says.

DANI AND I HAVE A ROUTINE THAT WE TRY TO FOLLOW ON NIGHTS WHEN work doesn't intervene.

She's an event planner, and events often happen at night, so her job probably gets in the way more than mine does. But when we're both home and available, we know what we're going to do without even having to discuss it.

We go out to dinner first. That's sort of a survival/self-preservation move, since between us there is not a single decent cook. If we had to eat at home, we'd starve. Something about inedible food is simply not appetizing.

After dinner we head home and watch a movie together on television. The choices are endless, and that's without even resorting to streaming. It's just never necessary; there is always something on regular television to watch.

The only problem with the routine, and it's fairly significant, is that Dani chooses the movies. Unfortunately, she only picks what could be described as "sensitive" movies; I can't re-member the last time I saw an explosion in one of them, other than the emotional kind.

Actually, I think it's the title that matters to her more than the movie. If the *Terminator* movie was titled *End of the Beating Heart,* Dani would watch it and might even like it.

She also likes older movies and has a weird bias that the older the film, the better. I think she's confusing it with wine and wisdom; I don't see aging as necessarily being a positive in movies.

Tonight we're watching *Peggy Sue Got Married*, which will never be confused with *Platoon* or *Nightmare on Elm Street*. But it's pretty good, and it hits home with me.

Kathleen Turner plays a recently divorced woman who goes back in time to high school and is thus given the chance to do things differently based on how her life turned out. She can change her destiny if she wants to make different choices from the ones she originally made.

This is the cinematic version of my rebooting fantasy about the last few months of Jimmy Dietrich's life. When it's over, I tell Dani about what I've been thinking. It's the closest I've ever come to talking about my "feelings," and I'm not all that comfortable with it.

"Corey, you're not that powerful," she says.

"What does that mean?"

"You think you could have changed the direction of Jim-my's life with another couple of phone calls or maybe stopping over at his house for a talk? I know you try to fix things, that's your thing and it's a great quality, but there are limitations to what one person can do, even you."

"Haven't you ever wanted to go back and change some-thing? Something you regretted?"

"Not very often, although I certainly would pick a different caterer for the Hoffman wedding than the one that served bad shrimp."

I laugh. "That didn't work out?"

"The bride walked down the aisle, but there was no one to give her away. Everybody was on line for the bathroom."

Another laugh from me. "But the ceremony went forward?"

"I think so, but I'm not sure; I was third in line at the time."

The phone rings, and I pick it up; it's Laurie. "Sam has a report to give us on the restaurant. He referred to it as a 'partial.'"

"Did he say whether he came up with anything good?"

"He didn't say one way or the other, but he probably thinks so. He wants us to hear it in person, rather than over the phone. Sam likes to give good news face-to-face. And if it wasn't good, he wouldn't be rushing to provide a 'partial.'"

Sam is going to be at Laurie's at 10:00 A.M., so I say that I'll be there as well. I tell Dani about the conversation when I get off the phone.

"Sounds promising," she says. "Let the reboot begin."

"What do you mean?"

"This is your chance to fix things, Corey. You didn't have the power to save your friend, but if I know you, you can sure as hell find his killer."

MARCUS DOESN'T SHOW FOR THE 10:00 A.M. MEETING WITH SAM. MARCUS had told Laurie that he wasn't coming, which is not unusual.

He knows that we'll update him on anything he needs to know, and he'd rather be out on the street investigating than sitting in a den listening to Sam.

"So the restaurant came through with the reservations list for that night," Sam says. "I'll email it to both of you, but I brought hard copies as well. There are sixteen tables in the restaurant, and they basically have two seatings, so a total of thirty-two possibilities if they were full.

"There were twenty-six reserved tables that night, but of course there's no guarantee that people didn't show up without a reservation. So I have the twenty-six names and phone numbers, as well as the number of people in each party. But we can probably eliminate the five reservations prior to six P.M., maybe even as late as seven P.M., based on when Avery got to the parking spot."

"Do they validate parking?" I ask.

Sam shakes his head. "No, I looked into that. The parking lot near where Avery was parked is free to patrons of the restaurant, but there is no computer record of who parked there."

The more Sam says, the more I realize how difficult this is going to be. "Do they get a lot of walk-ins? Or is it all by reservation?"

"I asked that when I was there. It's mostly reservations, but not all. And he said they also sometimes get people who show up and eat at the bar."

As Sam is talking, Laurie and I make eye contact. I'm pretty sure she's thinking the same as I am: it seems like a long shot that anything can come out of this.

"So what are you doing next?" I ask.

"Two things. The restaurant claims not to have computer records of the credit card receipts from that night. That doesn't really make sense to me; but I also don't know why they would lie about it, unless they think it's protecting their customers somehow. I'm looking in their system to make sure they're telling the truth; if they are, then I'll have to get the information another way."

Neither Laurie nor I ask what that other way is; if we found out, we might feel compelled to tell him not to do it.

Sam continues, "Once I have that, I'll cross-check it against the reservations. Not everyone who made the reservation will have been the one to pay, so we'll get some more names that way."

"You said you were doing two things," I say.

Sam nods. "Right. I've started doing background checks on

the people on the reservation list. I'm doing a cursory check now because it's so time-consuming. If I come up with anything interesting, we can obviously dig deeper."

"Good."

"There's already one thing I found that I wanted to bring to your attention."

I don't have a mirror to know for sure, but I think my ears literally perk up at this. This could be what Laurie was talking about when she said that if Sam has any good news, he likes to reveal it in person. I see a small smile on Laurie's face, so I know she's thinking the same thing I am.

"Let's hear it," I say.

"Okay, there was a guy who made a reservation for two at eight o'clock. I don't yet know who he was with."

Since Danny Avery was killed at 8:41, whoever Sam is talking about would have been in the restaurant at that time.

"His name was George Hafner. I don't know that much about him yet. He lived in a studio apartment on the East Side of Manhattan, Seventy-fourth Street. Thirty-seven years old, not married and no children."

"Why is he interesting to us at this point?" Laurie asks.

"Because he's dead. He was murdered in a drive-by shooting in Queens three weeks after Danny Avery was killed."

"Sam, you're right," I say. "That is very interesting."

THE POLICE NEVER EXAMINED ANY POSSIBLE CONNECTION BETWEEN THE murders of Danny Avery and George Hafner.

That's because they never knew that George Hafner existed, and they never knew he existed because they never connected Danny Avery to the restaurant. They did not solicit a list of the patrons because Danny was parked so far down the street. And because they didn't know the names of the patrons, George Hafner never appeared on their radar.

They never corrected their mistake, or maybe it wasn't and we're heading down a dead end. We won't know until we know . . . if then.

I say all of this just based on the written investigative documents. As important as it is to write down everything on a case, some things in the minds of the detectives never make it onto paper. The only way I am going to find out what those missing things might be is to go right to the source.

Lieutenant Donnie Griffith was the lead detective on the Avery murder. I knew Griffith in passing when I was on the force, but since we were in different departments, we didn't have that much interaction. I asked Pete Stanton to set up a meeting to discuss the case, which is why I am back at the precinct this morning.

It always feels weird when I come back here. On the one hand it seems like I never left, especially when Simon is with me. This was my home for a lot of years. But at the same time it feels like it all took place in another lifetime.

This time I've brought Simon with me; he has more friends here than I do. He's greeted at the entrance like a conquering hero; it's like he's walking through a petting gauntlet. Because of this it takes us a while to work our way back to Griffith's office.

"You brought your dog?" Griffith asks when we enter. He is clearly unfamiliar with Simon's fame and career.

"Always; he's a better cop than I ever was."

Griffith nods. "Oh, I forgot . . . you were K-9."

"And proud of it."

We make some small talk about life in the department; Griffith has three years to go before retirement and is anxious for them to go by so he can get out of the life. "But not you? You couldn't completely walk away?"

"I'm not sure, but I'm glad I didn't have to try. Going private was the perfect transition for me. I've got my hand in it, but on my terms."

"So Pete said you wanted to talk about Danny Avery?"

"I do. As I'm sure he must have told you, we're taking a shot at it."

"Toughest and most frustrating case I ever had. We got nowhere; never so much as a decent lead."

I nod sympathetically. "I've gone through the murder book; I can imagine how aggravating it was for you. When it's a cop . . ." It's not the kind of sentence I have to finish.

"We spent months banging our heads against the wall. Now I guess it's your head and your wall. Have at it; I hope you get it done."

"Thanks. Tell me what's not in the book. Any instincts you had that maybe you couldn't confirm? Anything you heard that maybe wasn't credible enough to write down?"

He hesitates. Then, "If I didn't put it down, it's not worth saying."

"Or maybe it is."

Another hesitation. "We . . . I should say I . . . heard that Avery might have been dirty."

"Dirty how?" I'm surprised to hear this; it does not jibe with anything I have ever heard about Danny Avery.

"I don't know; I couldn't get it out of the guy. And it didn't connect with anything I knew about Avery, so there was no reason to put it in the book."

"What did this guy say?"

"That maybe Avery was playing both sides, and he couldn't navigate it, although I'm sure he wouldn't have used the word *navigate*. That the word was Avery got in with some bad people and maybe couldn't get out."

"Who was the guy?"

"Name is Vince Petri—a lowlife who used to work for Joseph Russo, Sr. Not exactly a highly credible source, which was another reason I didn't take it seriously."

The elder Russo ran a local, actually *the* local, crime family in North Jersey. When he got his head blown off, Joe Jr. took over. The younger Russo's head is at the moment still intact, but the day is young.

"Petri didn't move on to work for Joe Jr.?"

"Can't say for sure, but I don't think so. I think he's an independent contractor now. Maybe Russo does some of the contracting, but I couldn't confirm that either way."

"What did Petri do for Russo Sr.?"

"Whatever was necessary. Violence and probably murder was involved."

"Why was he on your radar in the Avery case?"

"He ran with Frank Gilmore, the guy Avery killed in that domestic violence thing. I was thinking Petri, based on his history, might have been evening the score."

"I thought Gilmore traveled in fancier circles." The story at the time was that Gilmore was wealthy, and something of a philanthropist.

Griffith nods. "Yes and no. He had plenty of money and was accepted in that world. But for fun he apparently liked the, shall we say, tawdrier element. Petri was one of them."

"You no longer think Petri might have done it?"

Griffith shrugs. "It wouldn't shock me if he did, but I couldn't make him for it for two reasons. First of all, he produced witnesses who said he was in a bar at the time of the shooting. Not ironclad, and they could have been lying or mistaken, but it would have been hard to make a case.

"Second, guys like Petri do things for money, not friendship. It's not like he and Gilmore were blood brothers. And Petri never struck me as the loyalty type."

"Did you believe him when he said Avery was dirty?"

"Let's just say it bugged me, the way he said it. Casually, like it wasn't a big deal to him. He had no reason to lie, but also he obviously was not the most trustworthy guy in the world."

"You know where I can find him?"

"No, but it wouldn't be hard. Just look under rocks."

"Anything else not in the book?"

Another hesitation. Then, "That incident where Avery shot and killed Gilmore . . ."

"What about it?"

"Avery was apparently bitter about how that went down afterwards. He was cleared by internal affairs and another independent investigation. But people say he thought the department hung him out to dry publicly and took away any real chance for promotions. He probably wasn't wrong about that either."

"You think that has something to do with his murder?"

Griffith shrugs. "Not necessarily. But if he had turned dirty, and I'm sure not saying he did, maybe that was a factor."

I can understand why Griffith is saying that, and I can also understand why it's not in the book. You don't accuse another cop of that, even indirectly, if you don't have the evidence. Rumors like that don't make it into the book.

"Do you think Avery could have been watching the restaurant, maybe waiting for someone to come out?"

Griffith looks surprised. "What restaurant? Marcella's?"

"Yes."

"Not where he was parked."

I decide not to share Andy's parking lot theory. "Did the name George Hafner ever come up?"

"I don't think so. Was it in the book?"

"No."

"Who is he?"

"He was eating dinner in the restaurant when Avery was killed."

"So?

"He was murdered three weeks later. Drive-by shooting in Queens."

Griffith does a near double take. "Is that right? Any ties to Avery?"

"Not yet, but we just found out about him. We're checking into it now."

"Sounds promising. I'd be real interested in hearing what you find out."

"You can count on it."

"Anybody who could sneak up and shoot someone in the head like that . . ."

It's another sentence that doesn't need to be finished.

FOR MOST OF MY LIFE, I DIDN'T HAVE TO DO ANYTHING TO STAY FIT.

Being in shape was my status quo. I did as much athletic stuff as my job would allow, usually basketball, racquetball, and tennis, but I did it because I enjoyed it, not to keep my stomach from edging out over my pants.

Now I still play basketball and racquetball whenever I can, and even though I enjoy it and it beats the hell out of running, I do it partly so Dani will stop referring to me as Mr. Chubs. It's a modest goal that I have set.

This morning I'm getting in a quick racquetball game with my friend Barry Immerman. The good news is that Barry is a doctor, so he can be here to provide CPR if I need it.

The bad news is that he is a much-better racquetball player than I am, so he runs me around the court, making it far more likely that I will need that CPR.

We always play to win two out of three games, though the

third game, sadly, is never necessary to crown a winner. Today he beats me 21–14 and 21–16. Scoring more than 10 points is a moral victory for me, so by that standard I'm on a two-game winning streak.

Barry has dispatched me quickly, so I'm able to shower, pick Simon up, and make it to Laurie's in plenty of time for a meeting.

Laurie, as is her custom, has made a bunch of pancakes for me and Sam, who has called the meeting to give us his latest information. She also has biscuits for Simon. I've had worse partners in my life than Laurie.

Once I've had enough pancakes to obliterate anything positive that might have come out of my racquetball exercise, Sam, Laurie, and I go into the den so Sam can update us on his progress, or lack of same.

"So in addition to the names of the twenty-one people who made reservations after six P.M., I now have twenty-six credit card records from that night," he says. "Like everything else, it's complicated. There could be some receipts from people who were walk-ins without a reservation, and in some cases more than one person might have paid the bill for a specific table. For example, they might have split it two or three ways."

"And some people could have paid cash," I say.

Sam nods. "Right. So it's a very inexact science, but it's the best I can do."

"It's terrific, Sam," Laurie says.

"I've started getting as much background information as I can on each of the names, but it's going to be a fairly long process. Also, I really don't know what I'm looking for; it doesn't seem likely I'll find something that will be a flashing light suggesting that a particular person is the one Avery might have been following."

"Just give us whatever information you come up with, and we'll go through it," I say.

Laurie nods her agreement. "The first thing we can do is find out if any of them have police records. I'll take care of that."

We long ago decided that Laurie is the best person to get information from the department. Hard as this is for me to comprehend, she is more likable than I am. The cops we're dealing with are all overworked with their own stuff, so they're not inclined to respond quickly to our requests.

Some of them might even be resentful of us, particularly if they find out what we're getting paid. Whatever the case, Laurie has a much better chance of getting results than I do.

"I have done some work on George Hafner, the guy who ate at the restaurant and then was killed three weeks later in Queens. Thirty-seven years old, never been married, has had a number of different jobs, but seems to have been unemployed when he died. And he does have a record."

"Conviction?" I ask.

"Yes, for passing bad checks. Sentenced to eighteen months, served eleven. Got out three years ago."

"Certainly worth looking carefully at him," I say. "I have a good contact pretty high up in NYPD; he'll get me in to see whoever we need to talk to."

"There's only one other thing I have," Sam says. "The restaurant lists table numbers next to the reservations, so we know that Hafner was at table number one. The receipts also show table numbers, and none are for that table."

"So whoever paid the bill paid in cash?"

"Probably. Unless he ran a tab there. But cash is more likely. There's also an *R* in parenthesis after Hafner's name on the reservation sheet, but I don't know what that means."

"Sam, is that parking lot exclusively for the restaurant?" Laurie asks.

"It's supposed to be, but there's certainly no guarantee. It's self-park with no ticket."

"So there's nothing to prevent a person who wasn't a restaurant patron from parking there?" I ask.

"Correct."

Laurie and I make eye contact; we are clearly saying to each other that this process is a very long shot. But that's okay; we've just started, and by definition cold cases are not easily solvable.

"So I'll be tracing these people," Sam says. "Anything else for me?"

"Actually, yes," I say. "Can you access phone records for Danny and Susan Avery, as well as Jimmy Dietrich, prior to their deaths? It would be good to know who they called and who called them. And maybe get their credit card records as well?"

"Sure." Sam would say "sure" if I asked him if he could make it to Mars in time for lunch. "How far back do you want to go?"

"Let's say six weeks before they died? Laurie?"

"Seems about right."

Sam nods. "Which is a bigger priority? The background checks or the phone and credit records?"

"Both," Laurie and I say simultaneously.

THE SECOND MURDER SCENE IS NOT GOING TO TELL US MUCH, ESPE-
cially since we don't actually know where it is.

All we know is that the bodies of Jimmy Dietrich and Susan Avery were found on Jimmy's boat, which was floating in
the ocean at the time. We don't know where the boat was when
they were killed, not that it would matter. But more important,
we don't even know if they were actually shot on the boat.

The closest Laurie and I can come is the dock where Jimmy
kept the boat, which is on City Island at the western end of
Long Island Sound. I've been there before since Jimmy took me
out on his boat at least three or four times.

The boat was Jimmy's passion; the thirty-five footer could
sleep three and even had a small kitchen. He bought it used
and completely overhauled it; I don't think he was ever happier
than when he was on that boat, and working on it was a labor
of love for him.

He used to say that it was his only escape from being a cop. I knew exactly what he meant; being a police officer, even if one loves it, can be so stressful and all-consuming as to be overwhelming. To find a place where you can shut it off is to be cherished.

He kept the boat at a private launch, and Laurie and I drive out there. There's a new bridge to City Island, built just a few years ago, and we hit almost no traffic getting out there.

The launch is empty; it's possible it's not yet been assigned to anyone else, or perhaps it has and that person's boat is out on the water. I don't know what has happened to Jimmy's boat; possibly the police still have it impounded somewhere as evidence.

I should check on that. My guess is that Jimmy's will left everything to Caroline, and if that's the case, she'd be entitled to the boat to sell or do with as she pleases.

Laurie says, "I don't see any security cameras. There were a few near the main building, but none out here. So there is no way to know if they got on the boat themselves or were with someone else."

"None of this makes sense."

"How so?"

"Well, there are two possibilities to consider. The first, and in my mind the least likely, is a murder-suicide. Why come out on the boat to do it? He could have done it in his apartment or backyard, or Eastside Park or anywhere. Why come all the way out to City Island?"

"True."

"But the other scenario makes just as little sense. If someone was going to kill them, why bring them all the way out here? Why force them onto the boat? Jimmy was a tough guy; the longer he was in their control, the more chance he would have had to turn the tables."

"Maybe they were already dead before they were brought here."

I shake my head. "Jimmy's car was left here; it did not have any blood in it."

"It could be the idea was to let the weather at sea cover up what they did."

I ask what she means, but I already know what she's getting at.

She explains, "According to the murder book, the boat was here earlier the day before, so it must have been taken out late afternoon or at night. There was rain and wind that night, and it had been predicted. So the killers could have been counting on that to wipe away evidence of their involvement."

I nod. "Including the lack of gunpowder residue on Jimmy's hands. If that wasn't there, it would have made a suicide an impossibility. But since the elements would have washed it away, suicide stayed in play. The boat was out there for two days before the Coast Guard happened upon it; nobody reported either the boat or Susan and Jimmy missing."

"But if Jimmy committed suicide and didn't want people to know it, he could also have been counting on the weather to wash the evidence away."

Laurie's right, though I don't want to admit it. It seems like everything about this case has more than one possible explanation.

"You said Jimmy loved this boat?" she asks.

"Totally and completely. And he was proud of it."

"There could have been some psychological thing going on. Maybe on some level he wanted to die on it. Or maybe he didn't know for sure what he wanted to do until they were out on the water."

I shake my head. "I don't believe it; that's just not Jimmy.

But let's say you're right. Why include Susan Avery? Why add murder to the process?"

"I can't answer that, Corey. We know almost nothing about their relationship. She could have rejected him and it pushed him over the edge. Or maybe she was so distraught over Danny's death that she was the instigator of the plan.

"Maybe they both decided they had nothing to live for. It could be that she signed on for all of it. That would mean that while he technically murdered her, it was really a double suicide."

I don't bother telling Laurie that I don't buy it; she knows that already.

"Corey, let's go with the version you think it is, okay? The killers brought them out here that night, and they forced them onto the boat. Two days later, the boat is boarded by the Coast Guard out in the ocean, and the bodies are found."

I can anticipate her question. "How did the killers get back?"

She nods. "Exactly."

"Maybe they had another boat out there that picked them up."

"Seems like a lot of trouble for them to go to when they could have killed them anywhere."

"Not if they wanted it to look like a murder-suicide."

My argument has a hundred holes, but Laurie is nice enough not to point out any of them. She knows that I am aware of all of them, but I don't want to have to say so out loud.

"Let's go back to the house, Corey."

So we go back to the house. As expected, we know as much now as we did before coming here.

Which ain't a hell of a lot.

I ONCE PLAYED TENNIS AT THE WEST SIDE TENNIS CLUB IN FOREST HILLS, Queens. I'll never forget it.

A friend of mine in high school had a friend whose parents were members, and we were invited to play there. The match itself was uneventful, and I don't recall playing particularly well.

What made the experience memorable was the knowledge that the US Open had been played there for many years. They used to play it on grass, like Wimbledon, but then switched to a hard court surface. In the late seventies the event just became too big for the club to handle, and they built the National Tennis Center in Flushing. Since then it has become a mega-event.

So there I was, playing where guys like Laver and Emerson had played. It probably wasn't literally on the same court, but that didn't matter. It was the same location; I was occupying the same place on the planet and breathing the same air, albeit decades later.

So what if my serve couldn't break a pane of glass?

I take a short detour just to drive by the club, in a sudden uncharacteristic concession to nostalgia. It's only a few blocks from my destination on Continental Avenue, where I'm meeting with Lieutenant Corey Sewald of the NYPD Robbery-Homicide Division.

Lieutenant Sewald quickly agreed to see me when I told him I was investigating the murder of a cop. Playing this card works with somewhere in the neighborhood of 100 percent of cops anywhere, and I had no reluctance to play it because it is true.

Sewald's appearance and demeanor sort of define the term *grizzled veteran*. But he has a surprisingly warm smile and makes sure I have coffee as soon as I sit down.

Cop courtesy, even though I'm not a cop.

"So you turned in your badge?" he says, obviously having been prepped.

"I did, and haven't looked back. Except occasionally."

"I'm ready to pull the trigger on it myself. Or at least my wife is."

"It's worked for me, but I know people who have had the opposite experience," I say, thinking about Jimmy Dietrich. "And I've kept my hand in it, so withdrawal has been easier."

"Yeah," he says, seemingly lost in thought. I hope this guy makes the right decision. Then, as if suddenly remembering I'm sitting across from him, he says, "So what are you doing here?"

"A name has come up in connection with a case I'm working on. The case is the murder of a Paterson, New Jersey, cop two years ago, and the name is George Hafner."

"I pulled the Hafner hit. As you already know."

"That's why I'm here. You called it a 'hit.' A professional hit?"

"No question."

"It was a drive-by. Is there any chance Hafner wasn't the target?"

"None . . . one shot right in the heart. Nobody else was around. The shooter took his time and didn't miss. But if you think you can make Hafner for your cop killing, there's no way. Not his style."

"No, he's one of the few people on the planet that has an alibi for that night. He was having dinner in a restaurant at the time. But he might be involved in some other way. What can you tell me about him?"

"He's a loser, or I should say he *was* a loser. Did time for passing bad checks, but basically he was a con man. You want a fake ID, you go to him. You want someone to run a phone scam, he was your man. Actually, he was talented at what he did."

"He was in Paterson, New Jersey, three weeks before he died."

"So? Maybe he was swindling a cousin in New Jersey."

"The cop who was killed, Danny Avery, was watching the restaurant that Hafner was having dinner in when Avery was shot." I'm overstating it; we obviously don't know for sure that Avery was actually watching the restaurant.

"And that proves what?"

"Absolutely nothing. But Hafner getting killed a few weeks later at least makes him someone worth checking out."

"Agreed."

"Who can I talk to that knew Hafner well? Was he working at the time he was killed?"

"That's an interesting question. Hafner had a bunch of jobs; he didn't last long at any of them, but his scamming obviously wasn't providing enough food and shelter. But the four months before he died, he wasn't working."

"Where was he getting money?"

"Beats the hell out of me."

"I need to know who to talk to. Can I get a copy of your file on him?"

Sewald shakes his head. "No can do. You're technically a civilian. My captain would kill me."

"I understand. It can go to Paterson PD. Captain Pete Stanton, Homicide Division."

He nods. "I can do that."

"Great. So bottom line, any theories on who killed him?"

Sewald shrugs. "Somebody he pissed off. Hafner was a walking piss-off."

"You said it was a professional hit. What about Hafner would have made those kind of people kill him?"

"I don't . . ." Sewald stops, as if trying to decide whether to go further. Then, "I'm going to tell you something. I'm not supposed to know it myself, but after all my time here, nothing gets by without me knowing it."

"Okay."

"But if you tell anyone where you heard it, I will frame you for the goddamn Kennedy assassination. I'll make you as the second shooter from the grassy knoll."

"I was born decades too late, but I understand your position."

"About two weeks after Hafner bought it, Homeland Security pulled his file."

"Pulled his file?"

"Got my captain to send it to them. Actually, that's not

entirely true. They got the police commissioner to tell the police chief to tell my captain to send them a copy of the file."

"But you don't know why?"

"I don't have the slightest idea. If Hafner was a threat to our national security, our nation is in deep shit."

AT THIS POINT, HOMELAND SECURITY PULLING HAFNER'S FILE IS MORE interesting than important to us.

We don't know what was going on in Hafner's life, but to say that whatever it was also involved Danny Avery is beyond a stretch, at least at this point.

We don't even know for sure that Avery was watching the restaurant. If he was, we certainly don't know whether George Hafner was the reason. If George Hafner was the reason, we definitely don't know whether it had anything to do with Hafner's involvement with Homeland Security.

But it's an interesting twist, and a new development, which is a plus. When working a cold case, it's always a good feeling to come up with something that isn't simply a rehash of what the original investigators covered.

Laurie thinks it's more significant than I do. "Look at it this way," she says. "Jimmy Dietrich was killed just a few months after Danny Avery, and our entire operating assumption is that the two must be related. Why not make the same assumption with Avery and Hafner?"

"Well, for one thing, Hafner wasn't killed along with Avery's wife. Jimmy was."

She nods. "Point taken. But Jimmy was no easy target. He was smart and savvy, and he could certainly handle himself. Anybody that got close enough to put a bullet in his head knew what they were doing. Probably a pro, just like whoever killed Hafner."

"Agreed. And I'm certainly not saying we don't do a full-court press on Hafner. We just need to go much deeper."

"I'll call Pete and tell him to expect the information on Hafner from NYPD. I should also be getting anything that exists on possible criminal records for the other patrons at the restaurant that night."

"I'm going to meet Julie Simonson," I say.

"Who is she?"

"Danny Avery shot and killed her boyfriend, Frank Gilmore, in the domestic violence incident. I told her I wanted to talk about it, and she agreed."

Laurie nods. "That should be fun."

"We could switch, if you'd like. I could go talk to Pete, and you could interview Ms. Simonson."

"Bye, Corey."

I take that to be a no, so I head off to my appointment. Julie Simonson works at a supermarket not far from Route 208 in Glen Rock. It's about a twenty-minute drive, and I get there right on time at one o'clock.

Once inside, I go to the information desk, and as I am about to ask the young woman behind the counter where Julie might be, I see that her name tag says JULIE. Right under that, it says MANAGER.

"I'm guessing that you're Julie. And that you're the manager."

She smiles a great smile. "What tipped you off? You're Mr. Douglas?"

"Corey."

"Hi, Corey. Give me a minute." She leaves the counter, goes over and talks to a guy in one of the aisles, and heads back with him. He takes her position behind the counter.

"Let's go," she says. "There's a diner down the block."

"Are you hungry?"

Another smile. "Why do you think I told you to come by at lunchtime?"

We walk down the street to a diner. The woman behind the cash register smiles and greets Julie by name; I've got a feeling that she has been here before.

We sit down and the waitress asks me what I want, even though I don't have a menu, so I say, "Hamburger." It seems like a likely item for a diner to have, and an unlikely one for them to screw up. She nods and walks away.

"She didn't ask you what you want," I point out.

Another smile. "She knows." Then, "I know you want to talk about Frank, so let's get it over with, if that's okay."

"I understand it's an unpleasant subject."

"And an embarrassing one. It wasn't that long ago, but I look back on it amazed that I put myself in that position."

"Were there warning signs before that night that Gilmore was violent?"

"Not really. But I guess I had a gut concern; there were some times he just seemed a little off, you know? He had a temper, and I knew that, but it had never been directed at me, and it was never violent. I guess I was infatuated with him and maybe thought that with me he would be what I wanted. He certainly took me to fancy places and bought me nice gifts."

She stops, probably mentally revisiting those days. Then, "I was a twenty-three-year-old idiot." She laughs. "Now I'm a twenty-five-year-old wise woman."

I know it happens far too frequently, but it's hard to picture this woman going through what she did. The photos from that night show her to have been bruised and battered.

"Can you describe what happened that night?"

She nods, reluctant but willing. "Frank drank quite a bit, but he had always been able to control it, and I never saw it as a problem. But that night he had way too much and was in a foul mood."

I interrupt, "You were living together?"

"No, but he stayed over sometimes. He lived in a fancy apartment in Fort Lee, but I was only there a couple of times. That night . . . I don't even remember what we argued about, but I must have said or done something to set him off because he hit me a bunch of times. That was the first time that had ever happened. I don't just mean with Frank; no one had ever hit me before. And then it went from horrible to worse."

"How?"

"He took out a gun. Until then I never even knew he carried one. I panicked."

"What did you do?"

"I grabbed a phone and ran into the bathroom and locked the door. I was scared to death because he was screaming at me through the door, and I knew that he could start shooting through it. He was like a maniac. I have never been that scared before or since."

The waitress brings our food, temporarily interrupting the story. I get my hamburger, and Julie gets what is obviously her regular salad, kale with extra grilled asparagus on top. I'm just glad I hadn't said, "I'll have whatever she's having."

Once the waitress leaves, Julie continues, "So I called nine one one and they were there really fast. I came out of the bathroom; I had seen myself in the mirror and looked like a mess." She smiles. "The fact that I was crying didn't make me any more presentable.

"Frank was telling them it was nothing, that I fell and hurt myself, but once they saw me they knew what the truth was. But Frank . . . it was like he turned off a switch . . . he seemed calm and in control. He was back to what I thought was the normal Frank. It actually was an amazing transformation."

Julie's tone as she speaks is as if she is in awe at what she is describing. She can't seem to believe that the person this happened to was herself.

"The police asked us if there was a weapon in the house, and he said no. That really pushed me over the edge. I had had enough, and I started screaming the truth, that he'd hit me and threatened me with the gun." She shakes her head at the recollection.

"What happened next?"

"One of the officers took me into the other room, while the other one, who turned out to be Detective Avery, stayed with Frank. The next thing I remember was a loud gunshot. The officer told me to wait there, and he took out his own gun and ran into the other room. I heard talking, but didn't know what they were saying.

"He came back in and told me to stay where I was, and when I asked him, he said that Frank had been shot. I'm embarrassed to say I wasn't sorry to hear it.

"Next thing I knew, the place was filled with police and medics. And that was it. They asked me for a statement and I gave it. Then I spent the next two months reading about myself in the paper."

"Tell me some more about Frank Gilmore, please." I know a lot from the police reports; Laurie had Pete send over the file on the incident. But I want to hear it directly from Julie.

"I'll try, but I'm not sure I ever really knew him. He was like two different people; there was the charming, generous side, but there was a quality to him . . . on some level he was a . . . do they still use the word *hoodlum* anymore?"

I smile. "I still hear it occasionally. What did it mean in this case?"

"He was just dangerous, beneath the surface, you know? I can look back and see that now."

"How did you two meet?"

"The old-fashioned way." She smiles. "At a bar. It was in one of those fancy New York bars, with a VIP section, which I guess was for big spenders, or celebrities. He was in there, and he saw me, and the next thing I knew I was a VIP. It was more intoxicating than the liquor."

"What kind of work did he do?"

"I don't know exactly, but he did not seem to have a job that he went to every day. Yet he always had plenty of money. I asked him once what he did, and he said something like 'Whatever is necessary.' But he smiled, so I thought he was joking around."

"Did you meet any of his friends?"

She nods. "A few; that's why I said 'hoodlum.' They seemed dangerous like Frank, but without the other, appealing side. I just couldn't picture Frank being comfortable with them, but he obviously was. That should have scared me away, but it didn't."

"Do you know any of their names?"

"No, I just don't remember. I'd probably recognize them, though. For some strange reason I am much better with faces than names. I also briefly met a couple of people at Frank's apartment; I think they were businesspeople. I don't know their names either."

"Does the name Vince Petri ring a bell?" Petri is the guy who told Lieutenant Griffith that the word was that Danny Avery was "dirty." Griffith had spoken to him because he was said to be an associate of the guy Avery shot, Frank Gilmore.

Griffith also said that Petri was dangerous and used to work for Joseph Russo, Sr. We already have Marcus out looking for Petri; when he finds him, Marcus will arrange a conversation. Marcus is really good at arranging conversations.

"The name sounds familiar, but I can't be sure," Julie says.

"So you have not been in touch with anyone you met through Gilmore since his death?"

"No. And I don't want to." Then she changes the subject to something she considers more pleasant. "They make the best kale salad here."

"I'm sure it must be wonderful. It's so hard to find tasty kale these days."

I PUT ON MY MOST NONDESCRIPT SUIT, WHICH IS ALSO MY ONLY SUIT, and go down to Marcella's Restaurant.

I do this so that the manager of the restaurant will think I'm a cop, without me explicitly telling him that I'm a cop. Impersonating a police officer is a law I am not inclined to break. Dressing like one is fine.

When I get to the restaurant, I ask the bartender where the manager is. I say that I am working for the Paterson Police Department, which is technically true. He heads to the back to tell the manager that I'm here.

They come back out together, and the guy who is obviously the manager says, "I'm Adam Kramer; I'm the manager. Officer . . . ?"

"Detective." I leave out the word *private*. "Douglas. Corey Douglas. I would like to talk to you about this material you supplied to one of our people."

I take out a printout of the reservations from the night Danny Avery was killed. That I have it provides me with credibility that I am who I haven't said I am.

He is convinced. "How can I help, Detective?"

"Well, for starters, have you ever seen this man?" I show him a photograph of George Hafner that we got from the file that was sent to Pete by the Queens police.

Kramer looks at it for a few moments. "I don't recall if I did."

"He ate here about two years ago, the night of the murder down the street."

"I'm sorry, Detective, but I'm sure you understand that a lot of people come in here. I try and remember faces, but this one doesn't register. He certainly was not a frequent customer."

"He ate at table number one, and we're trying to determine who he might have eaten with."

I see a reaction from Kramer when I mention table number one, but he seems to recover quickly and shakes his head. "I'm afraid we have no way of finding out who that was."

"I understand. Where is table one?"

He points to a table in the back of the restaurant, in the far corner. "That one over there. That's number one, then number two, and so forth as you go down the row along the window. Then it loops around."

"There's an R in parentheses after George Hafner's name. What would that stand for?"

"I'm afraid I have no idea."

"Who would have taken the reservation?"

"There's no way to tell; we've had a number of people come through here. You know how it is; everybody always thinks they can make more money and have a better career at the next stop." Kramer frowns. "Welcome to the restaurant business."

"I'm sure it's a tough business. Is that a highly sought-after table?"

"What do you mean?"

"Well, it's private and well positioned. Frank Sinatra used to say that he wanted that kind of table, so he could see everyone that came in; he didn't want to be surprised. That table would fit the bill."

Kramer smiles. "Mr. Sinatra, if he was still with us, could have any table he wanted. But in our case it is first come, first served."

I thank him and leave. As soon as I get the car started and pull out, I call Sam. He answers on the first ring, as always, with "Talk to me."

"Sam, I need you to do something. When I mentioned the fact that Hafner was at table number one, the manager reacted and then covered it up."

"So?"

"So, can you get into the reservation records for maybe a couple of months around the time of the murder. I want to know if there's a person who seems to be a regular at that table. If there is, see if he still goes there."

"Will do, but remember Hafner made the reservation. If that is standard practice, then whoever you are looking for won't show up on the sheet. It would always be who he was eating with."

"I understand, but it's worth a shot. Please make it a priority."

"You got it."

I call Laurie to update her on what I've learned, which doesn't take long because I basically haven't learned anything.

She has some welcome news for me, though. "Marcus found Vince Petri."

"Excellent. We need to talk to him; can Marcus set it up?"

"I don't think Petri is willingly doing interviews, but Marcus knows where he lives. He thinks an unannounced visit might be in order."

"Agreed. You okay if I make the visit?"

"Sure."

What we don't bother saying is that whichever of us goes, we will be accompanied by Marcus. As ex-cops used to being in tough situations, both Laurie and I can handle ourselves quite well. But we are not in Marcus's league, so we almost always let him lead the way.

We have been alerted that Petri is dangerous, that he was an enforcer of sorts for Joseph Russo, Sr. He won't be expecting us, and it's possible he's not big on surprises.

But he's in for a big one.

"IF R STANDS FOR A PERSON, THEN TABLE NUMBER ONE IS HIS REGULAR table," Sam says. "Because a lot of the reservations for that table have an R after the person's name. Not all of them, but most."

"You think *R* may not be a person?" Laurie asks.

Sam shrugs. "I have no idea. Maybe the letter is specific to that table; maybe a waiter named Rudolph always takes care of it. But there is no letter designation on any other reservations for any other tables."

"But *R* doesn't make the reservations? Someone else does?" I ask.

"Actually, not always. On quite a few of the nights, it just has the letter *R* with no other name. The reservations in those cases is for one person."

"So if *R* is a person, and he dined with Hafner while Avery was watching, then we need to know who he is," Laurie says.

"I've got good news on that front," Sam says. "The reservation for tonight at that table just says *R*. So maybe our boy is eating alone."

"Terrific," I say. "We go there tonight, check him out, and follow him. All we need is to get his license plate number when he leaves."

"Not 'we,'" Laurie says. "You were there today; the manager knows you and you asked about that table. We can't overplay our hand on this. It has to be me."

I just nod; there's no sense arguing since she's absolutely right.

Laurie calls out, "Andy!"

Andy comes in from the other room. "Let me guess, you want me to make another unreimbursed pizza run."

"A woman cannot live by pizza alone, hubby. Tonight you are taking me to a nice dinner. We're going to Marcella's . . . it has to do with the case."

"Did you say tonight?" he asks, clearly not pleased.

"Yes. You had other plans?"

"I did. Today is Monday, so tonight is Monday night. You may not be aware of this, but Monday is the night they play *Monday Night Football*. The Giants are playing San Francisco."

"So tape it and watch it tomorrow. For one week only it will be *Tuesday Night Football*."

"That's not how it works. Once the game is played, it's played. I'll know the score. The Giants will have lost, so I won't want to watch it."

Andy is aware that Laurie knows all this, and he is also very aware that he's not going to win this argument.

He takes one last shot at it and turns to me. "Why don't you two go to dinner? You can talk about the case and have a blast."

I shake my head. "Marcus and I will be questioning a guy who used to be an enforcer for Joseph Russo. You want to switch places?"

Andy turns to Laurie. "We'll have a lovely dinner."

THE TWO BUILDINGS THAT COMPRISE THE MODERN MAY WELL BE THE TWO fanciest apartment buildings in New Jersey.

They both tower forty-seven stories above Fort Lee, providing an amazing view of New York City, across the Hudson River.

Frank Gilmore lived there before he met an untimely death at the hand of Danny Avery, minutes after Gilmore beat up Julie Simonson and threatened her with a gun.

I don't have a good feel for who Gilmore was, and I think it's important that I change that, which is why I'm here at the Modern.

Gilmore seemed to lead a double life. He lived in a luxurious place like this, among the affluent. But then Detective Griffith and Julie Simonson both told me he also hung out with a very different group, the type of people who the residents here would call the police on if they found them standing in the lobby.

After Gilmore's death, newspaper reports described him as something of a philanthropist, donating to various charitable causes, including some benefiting rank-and-file police groups. That certainly contributed to the controversy when Danny Avery sent him to that great apartment building in the sky.

The good news is that I know the manager of this building from my days on the force. They had two robberies, inside jobs, which I solved. So the on-site manager, Scott Quinn, and I are buddies of sorts.

I called him and he was helpful in arranging an interview with Gilmore's across-the-hall neighbor, Cynthia Yarborough. He had asked around and apparently she knew him best among the people in the building, although Quinn cautioned me that Yarborough and Gilmore were not exactly "best buddies."

I leave Simon at home since I'm not sure how Yarborough would feel about a dog in her apartment. The doorman calls up and clears my entrance, and as soon as Yarborough opens her eighteenth-floor apartment door, I regret not bringing Simon along.

She has two of the best-looking golden retrievers I have ever seen. One is gold and one is cream colored, and knowing Simon as I do, he would be crazy about them.

Maybe next time.

We say hello, and we give each other permission to call each other by our first names. Cynthia seems nice enough, but my initial focus is on the two goldens; they are rather difficult to stop petting. Fortunately, I have as many hands as there are golden heads.

Finally we're seated, and she says, "I understand from Scott that you want to talk about Frank Gilmore."

"Right. He lived right across the hall?"

"Yes, but if you've ever lived in an apartment building like this . . . well, living nearby doesn't make us neighbors in the way one would ordinarily think about the concept. We don't exactly have block parties or watch the kids playing tag in the street. Usually the most we do is nod on elevators. Sometimes we mumble good morning."

"I understand. But you knew Gilmore?"

"Not well, but we used to borrow things from each other."

"What kind of things?"

"Nothing important. My ice maker wasn't working once, and he came to the rescue. I remember he borrowed a hammer from me when he was hanging pictures . . . that kind of thing."

"What was your impression of him?"

"Always seemed nice enough. I know neighbors of criminals always say that, but in this case it's true. I was a bit shaken up when I saw what happened to him. You know, what he was accused of doing that night."

"What else did you know about him?"

"I have a friend who is a fundraiser for some charities. She said that Frank was a semi-reliable contributor, but he didn't want to volunteer his time as well. Just money, which was fine."

I've heard about his charitable contributions before, and Laurie is out today interviewing some of the executives from the charities he donated to.

"Ever see any of his friends?" I ask.

"Never. I never saw anyone come to his apartment either. That doesn't mean it didn't happen; I just didn't see it."

"So is it fair to say you were shocked when you saw the domestic violence allegation the night he was killed?"

"Stunned. Everybody here was; it actually got people

talking on the elevator and in the lobby." She smiles. "So in a way he brought people together."

I return the smile. "I'm sure he would have been thrilled to hear it."

"But it didn't last. We're back to nodding."

LAURIE AND ANDY ARRIVED RIGHT ON TIME FOR THEIR SEVEN O'CLOCK reservation.

They didn't make a specific table request; that wasn't necessary because table number one can be seen from everywhere in the restaurant. Number one had one table setting on it, which seemed consistent with Sam's assessment of the reservation.

The plan was for Laurie and Andy to finish eating when R was midmeal, then go sit in their car, which was parked across the street. When R came out, they would follow him.

At eight fifteen, they were finishing their entrée, but table number one was still unoccupied. Andy looked at his watch. "Kickoff is in five minutes. If we hurry—"

Laurie interrupted, "He's here."

A tall man who looked to be in his forties, wearing a suit and tie, was led to table number one. Other members of the staff greeted him, and he smiled and nodded to them. They were obviously treating him with deference.

He was not given a menu, but the waiter quickly came over to take his order. This guy had clearly been to this restaurant quite a few times, and one of those times was with George Hafner.

Once Laurie and Andy got a good look at him, they no longer had any reason to stare. Instead they went back to their meal, ordering dessert and coffee. They were in no hurry; as long as they left before the man at table one, they were fine.

The man, probably R, ordered a drink, then had a shrimp cocktail. When his entrée arrived, Andy paid the check, and he and Laurie went outside to sit in the car and wait. Laurie got in the driver's seat, since she had far more experience following someone than Andy did.

They were considerably closer to the restaurant than Avery had been that night, and they could clearly see anyone coming out.

They sat in silence for a few minutes, until Laurie said, "You could turn the football game on the radio if you want."

"No thanks." Andy adjusted the rearview mirror.

"Why?"

"The last person we know of who waited in the dark for someone to come out of that restaurant wound up with a tag on his toe. I want us to be able to hear anyone who might be approaching."

"Good point."

An hour later, they were still waiting. "How can a guy eating alone take this long?" Andy asked. "If it was me, I would have ordered something to go."

"If it was you, you'd be home watching the Giants game."

Just then a large black sedan pulled up and parked in front

of the restaurant. A chauffeur got out and waited next to the car. The guy from table one came out a few minutes later, and the chauffeur opened the back door and let him in.

They drove off, and after waiting for fifteen seconds, Laurie pulled out behind them. This was not a high-risk situation; there was little reason to think that the chauffeur would be alert to the possibility of being followed.

But since they knew little about the situation, including who was sitting in the backseat of the sedan, Laurie was careful not to attract attention. She was practiced at it, having done a great deal of this kind of surveillance when she was a cop.

They were going to have to follow R wherever he was going; getting the license plate would now not be sufficient. The car might have been hired for the evening, which would mean it was not in R's name. Nevertheless, Laurie planned to get the license plate later, so Sam might be able to trace it in the limo company's computer.

They drove for more than thirty minutes to Short Hills, an affluent community southwest of Paterson. It became a little trickier for Laurie then, as far fewer cars were on the darkened street, so it would be easier to notice them.

The sedan ultimately pulled into a long, winding driveway leading up to an impressive home. Andy noted the address as they passed by, and Laurie pulled over a quarter of a mile past the house.

It was fifty-fifty that the sedan would exit past them, and if it did, they could get the license plate then. After just a few minutes, which would have been enough time for R to get dropped off, the sedan did, in fact, head their way. Andy snapped a photo of the license plate.

Laurie waited for the sedan to get well out of range before she started the car and pulled away. As soon as she did, she called Sam and asked him to check on the house address, as well as the sedan license plate.

When she got off the phone, Andy turned the football game on the radio.

The announcer said, "It's been a rough first half for the Giants, as they trail the Forty-Niners, twenty-four to six."

"Doesn't sound like you missed much," Laurie said.

ACCORDING TO MARCUS, VINCE PETRI HAS NO APPARENT LEGAL SOURCE of income, at least not one that involves having a job.

Yet he lives in a fairly expensive house in an upscale Ridgewood neighborhood; Marcus followed him there the other night.

Marcus was in favor of confronting him in his house, but I vetoed the idea. If Petri does not want to talk to us and we force our way in, that would be breaking and entering at worst and illegal trespassing at best. I make it a habit to try to avoid breaking laws that I spent twenty-five years enforcing.

Marcus's research showed that Petri went to one place almost every night, and it wasn't the opera or ballet or library. It was a bar in Passaic called Happy's. I'd heard of it because a few months ago a brawl out front resulted in a shooting death, and the television commentator reporting on it speculated that the bar might consider a new name.

On the nights Marcus had observed, Petri had left the bar about midnight, one hour before its closing time. Sometimes he left with friends; one time he was alone. The friends were always men about his age; Happy's did not seem to be a place one frequented to pick up women. Drinking and talking, along with the occasional fighting and shooting, seemed to be the main sources of amusement.

If we have a plan tonight, it's loose, flexible. We will show up at eleven o'clock and wait down the block from the bar in the direction that Petri walks to his car. We will intercept him there, whether or not he is alone.

If we miss him, if for some reason he didn't show up or left early, or if he walks in a different direction, that's okay. This mission is not particularly time sensitive; if we talk to Petri tomorrow or the day after that, it's fine. One of the few advantages of working on cold cases is that there is rarely a need to strike while they are hot.

Where we are waiting for Petri is quite dark, and we are standing against the side of a building. Petri will not likely see us until he is almost upon us. I've brought Simon with us; he has been trained to look extremely intimidating when the situation calls for it. He is the Marcus of police dogs.

Not until 12:10 do we hear people coming toward us. If it's Petri, he's not alone; I can make out at least three and maybe four voices. They are the first voices I've heard since we got here; Marcus has characteristically not said a word. That's fine; I like it when he's focused.

Marcus nods to me, a silent confirmation that we are going forward despite the additional people. I'm not surprised; if Petri was leading a North Korean marine battalion, Marcus would be confident that he could handle them.

And he'd be right.

"Petri," I say, as soon as we see them, and before they realize that we are there.

His response, and that of his three colleagues, is aggressive. "Who wants to know?" he asks, as the group moves toward us in a confident, threatening manner. I'm assuming that the guy who asked the question is Petri; I don't know what he looks like. Marcus does, though, so there's no chance we will wind up with the wrong guy.

As Petri gets close, Simon tenses and growls, causing Petri to come to a full stop. "Whoa. Watch your dog."

"You'd better watch my dog before he mistakes you for a soupbone."

"What's this about?"

"We want to talk to you about Danny Avery."

It's been almost two years since Avery was killed, and since Petri has claimed not to have been involved, I would have thought the name might take a moment to place. But Petri's response is not "Who's Danny Avery?"

Instead it's "Get lost."

"You're missing the point. You're going to talk to us. Whether you do it voluntarily or not is your choice."

If he's intimidated, he's hiding it well. "Beat it, losers. Take your dog and go home, before you get hurt."

"Okay, here's the situation; try your best to follow along. We simply want to talk to you. When I am finished with this verbal paragraph, you will have ten seconds to decide whether you want to do it standing up or flat on your back. The clock starts now."

Apparently they make a group decision to go with "standing up" because they move toward us, as one. I won't say it's synchronized, but they all seem to make the decision at the same time.

The only word I say is "Stay," alerting Simon that he should sit this one out until called upon.

Marcus and I haven't planned this out in advance, but an observer might think we had, since we act in a coordinated fashion. I punch Petri in the gut, a short punch designed to stun and deprive him of any oxygen that might have been hanging out in his lungs.

He bends over, gasping and in pain, and I follow it with a right cross to his left temple. I don't hit him with full force because I don't want to hurt my hand, and if Petri is unconscious, it will hamper his ability to converse, which is why we're here in the first place.

Marcus is meanwhile dealing with Petri's friends, and he has no such desire to hold back. I can't see what he's doing because I'm dealing with Petri, but I hear some moaning and gasping, none of which seems to be coming from Marcus.

Once Petri has been deposited on the ground, I can see that he has joined two of his friends in that position. They are one on top of the other, with Petri the farthest off the ground. A good name for it would be Loser Mountain.

They are not moving, and it appears that Petri is the only member of the trio who is currently conscious. The fourth guy in the group is definitely moving; he is running down the street. He is obviously carrying with him the only brains in the entire outfit.

Simon looks annoyed that he has not been able to get in on the fun. This is going to cost me some biscuits later.

Marcus quickly frisks the three fallen heroes, taking a gun from both Petri and one of the others. I see that Petri's weapon of choice is a .38; Danny Avery was killed with a .38.

I lean down to help Petri to his feet. "Come on, we'll take you home. You shouldn't drive in this condition."

MARCUS DRIVES, WITH SIMON IN THE FRONT PASSENGER SEAT. I'M IN THE
back with Petri, who has quickly regained his surliness.

I'm assuming that's his natural state. As a former enforcer
for Joseph Russo, he must not be used to being manhandled like
this, but he's showing more anger than embarrassment.

"Where the hell are we going?"

"I told you. We're taking you home."

"You know where that is?"

"We know everything, including the fact that you killed
Danny Avery."

"That's bullshit. I have five witnesses that said I was drinking in that bar when he got whacked."

"They were lying, and you're lying. You were getting revenge for your friend, who beat up his girlfriend." I almost
called her by her name, Julie Simonson, but I caught myself. I
don't want her involved in this any further.

"No way. That ain't my way. I don't hit women."

That was a total non sequitur, so I choose to ignore it. "I forgot; you're an extremely honorable man. What did you do for Joseph Russo?"

"Whatever needed to be done. But I don't work for him no more."

"Where do you get your money?"

"I do stuff. But I didn't hit Avery."

"Then who did?"

"I don't know, but he was dirty. He got in with the wrong people."

Petri is just repeating what he told the police in the original investigation. "What does that mean? Which people?"

"I don't know. I just heard things, after he got killed, that he was dirty and got in over his head."

"You're lying. You killed him."

"I got five witnesses that says I didn't."

"When we can prove that you did, five of your asshole friends won't be enough to protect you."

Having just seen what happened to him and his friends back on the street, he doesn't seem inclined to respond to that. Meanwhile, Marcus is pulling up to Petri's Ridgewood home.

"Get the hell out of the car," I say.

"You'll be seeing me again" is his response.

"That will give us something to look forward to. But just remember: we know where you live."

Once Petri is out of the car, I ask, "Marcus, you think he killed Avery?"

"Could have." Those are literally the first words I have heard Marcus speak in two hours.

"Yeah," I agree. The whole purpose of the meeting tonight was to get a sense of Petri, and my sense is that he's a piece of garbage, and a dangerous one at that. "He could come after us. We embarrassed him."

"I'm good with that. Next time he'll get more than embarrassed."

I call Laurie, who told me she would be waiting up to hear how it went, and to update me on whether she and Andy accomplished anything at the restaurant.

I go first, telling her exactly what happened. Her response when I finish is "Sounds like you made yourself an enemy."

"That's what I told Marcus."

"Let me guess: he didn't panic at the thought of it."

"You know him quite well."

"I don't think you're exactly panicked either."

"You know me quite well. How did your romantic dinner go?"

"Mixed result. Andy's chicken parmigiana was fine; my Greek salad was a little chewy. But the tartuffe dessert was to die for."

"All's well that ends well. Any chance you saw the elusive Mr. R?"

"We did, and followed him home to Short Hills. Sam has the address and will be here in the morning to tell us all about him."

"What time?"

"Does nine o'clock work?"

"Pancakes?"

"As many as you can eat."

"Excellent. Simon and I will see you then."

DANI IS LEAVING TOWN THIS MORNING; SHE HAS A CLIENT IN MIAMI WHO is getting married, and Dani has planned the affair.

The caterer and all the other service people have been hired; Dani just wants to be on scene to make sure nothing goes wrong. Apparently a lot of unpleasant surprises can happen in the event-planning biz.

I wonder if she would plan our M, if we ever got M . . . ed.

On the way to dropping her off at Newark Airport, I tell her about the meeting with Petri last night. When she kisses me good-bye, she says, "Try not to get killed while I'm gone; my Match.com profile isn't current."

I'm not happy about her leaving, which is a recent but recurring phenomenon for me. Prior to Dani, I can't ever remember being in a relationship from which I wouldn't have welcomed at least a temporary break. Or a permanent one.

Simon is in the backseat, and Dani leans in to give him a

good-bye hug. That is just another of many reasons why she is perfect for me. If I ever wanted to M, and if she wanted to M, I couldn't make a better choice.

I get to Laurie's at eight thirty, and Sam is already there with his mouth full. True to her word, Laurie has made enough for both of us, and not until nine fifteen do we push away from the table and head into the den to hear what Sam has to say.

"R's name is Jacob Richardson. You already know where he lives in Short Hills, and that sedan was owned by a limousine company that he obviously hired for the night. He does own a car, actually two of them . . . a Lexus and an Audi. So for some reason he chose not to drive; I'll check the limo company's records to see if he uses them a lot.

"I've just got minimal background on him so far; I'll do a deeper dive starting later today. But he owns a company called JR Capital, with an office in Paramus. The website, such as it is, presents it as a company that invests in start-ups, mostly in the tech field.

"I haven't yet been able to determine which start-ups they have invested in, so I'll also try and get more information about that. I also haven't discovered any connection between Richardson and George Hafner, but I'm not sure there would be any way to do that. I'll certainly search for it."

"They had dinner together," I say. "That's connection number one."

Laurie and I pepper Sam with questions about Richardson, but he's already told us all he knows at the moment. Finally Laurie asks, "Anything else, Sam?"

He nods. "I've done some checking into the phone and credit card records of Danny Avery, Susan Avery, and Jimmy Dietrich in the weeks before they died." He holds up a folder.

"There's a lot of stuff, and it's all in here. It might mean more to you than it does to me."

"Anything jump out at you?" I ask.

"Not really, because I don't know what you're looking for. Though I was surprised to see that Dietrich stayed at a hotel in upstate New York on three different occasions in the last two months of his life. He'd also done some other traveling."

I'm surprised to hear that, and I say so.

Laurie says, "He could have been at the hotel with Susan Avery. If they were in fact having an affair, it would have been a good place to get some privacy."

I'm afraid I'm thinking the same thing, but Sam comes to the rescue. "I don't think so."

"Why not?" I ask.

"Well, first of all, the reservations say one adult, though of course that doesn't prove anything. More significantly, during two of the times Dietrich was at the hotel, Susan Avery made credit card purchases back here in New Jersey. Unless someone else was using her card and forged her signature, she wasn't at the hotel with Dietrich."

"Maybe he was with someone else," Laurie says, but I don't believe it. Just picking up and going to a hotel was not Jimmy's style. He was not vacationing; he had a reason for going.

"If he was having an affair, which I doubt, this still doesn't fit. Why drive all that distance? He and Caroline were heading to a mutually agreed divorce; who was he hiding from? And to go up there three times? There has to be another reason."

"So one of us needs to go there."

I nod. "I will; you have two children to take care of."

"You're right. Ricky's growing up; Andy isn't. He doesn't like to travel during football season."

"You got that right," Andy says, having just walked into the room. "It's one of the things that makes me a real man. Where is it we're not traveling to?"

"Upstate New York. Jimmy Dietrich went to a hotel there three times before he died."

"Alone?"

"We don't know yet," I say. "That's one of the things I'm going to find out."

"From the way you describe him, he doesn't sound like the type to be going on a singles weekend."

"He wasn't."

"Where are we on Vince Petri?" Laurie asks. "Could he have killed Avery?"

I nod. "It's definitely possible. For one thing, he didn't seem surprised when we asked about him. The murder was a long time ago; it felt like Petri shouldn't have so quickly recognized the name and what we were talking about. But more importantly, I never like to eliminate a murderer as a suspect in a murder case . . . and definitely not one with a revenge motive."

"Does he have an alibi?" Andy asks.

"Yeah. His friends say he was in a bar with them."

Andy frowns. "Let me guess . . . none of those friends are upstanding citizens that are beyond reproach."

"You can be sure of that." I turn back to Sam. "Anything else jump out at you?"

"Not sure if this means anything, but Susan Avery called a plastic surgeon's office three weeks before she died and paid him money."

"She had the surgery?" I ask.

"No, doesn't seem like it. She only paid him two hundred and forty bucks; maybe it was a consultation."

"Then no way she and Jimmy planned a double suicide,"

Andy says. "You don't consider plastic surgery if you're not planning to live a good long time."

"Plastic surgeons do much more than cosmetic things. I have a friend who went to one for breast reconstruction after a mastectomy. They also do hand surgeries, and a lot more," Laurie says.

I nod. "But the point still holds. You don't go to a doctor for almost any reason if you're planning to kill yourself."

"Exactly," Andy says. "Nobody washes a rental car."

I think I see Andy's point, but it's a strange reference, so I ignore it.

"Jimmy did not commit suicide, and he did not commit murder," I say.

I'm even starting to believe it.

LIEUTENANT SEWALD, THE QUEENS COP WHO WORKED THE HAFNER MURder, did as promised and sent a copy of the file to Pete.

Pete sent it on to me, and I was hoping to read something that would tell me why Homeland Security was interested in Hafner. Unfortunately, I don't see anything that would come close to explaining it.

However, the file does name a few close friends of Hafner's, and I'm heading to see one of them now. Unfortunately it means a trip back to Queens, and I'm no longer feeling the nostalgia necessary to visit the West Side Tennis Club again.

Sewald has done me the favor of calling the friend, Billy Miranda, and clearing the way for him to meet with me. He said that Miranda was reluctant, and Sewald had to use considerable powers of persuasion. Cops can be very persuasive when they want to be.

We're meeting in a small park in Flushing. I've gotten here

first, and from here I can see Citi Field in the distance, as well as the National Tennis Center. They are both more appealing places to be than sitting on this bench waiting for Billy Miranda.

I've brought Simon with me. I like to do that whenever I question someone I haven't met if I think that person might be resistant. They could have one of two reactions to seeing him. They could be intimidated, which would likely facilitate their talking. Or they could be dog people, in which case they'd warm up to me through Simon and also be more inclined to talk.

It's a win-win, especially since I like hanging out with Simon way more than with most people.

Miranda shows up and approaches hesitantly, not taking his eyes off Simon. He is firmly in the intimidated camp. He's probably early forties, thin, and hasn't shaved in a couple of days. He has not come here from teatime at the Plaza.

"Billy Miranda?"

"Yeah. Is he friendly?" He points to Simon.

"Unless he has reason not to be. Sit down."

Miranda cautiously sits on the edge of the bench, about as far from me and Simon as he can get. "Let's get this over with; that dog makes me nervous. The cop said you wanted to talk about George."

"He was a good friend of yours?"

"For a long time. Then, not so much."

"Why not?"

"Because he became hot shit, or at least he thought he did. I don't go for that crap."

"What does that mean?"

"He got in with some people that used him, gave him money, and then probably killed him."

"Who were those people?"

"I don't know and I don't want to know. George wouldn't

say, but he once told me they know everything and can do anything. They could even be watching us now." Miranda sounds
even more afraid of the unknown people than he is of Simon.

"You said they used him; what did you mean by that?"

"George was an asshole, and you couldn't trust him from
here to there. But I'm telling you, the guy was a genius."

"How so?"

"He just had a way about him. He could do anything. You
want an explosive? Give him a bottle of salad dressing, a tube
of toothpaste, and a match and he could blow up Citi Field. You
want a fake driver's license? George was your man. You want to
scam an old lady out of her life savings? Go to George."

Miranda seems to be warming to the topic. "But at the end
of the day, he got nowhere; everything he ever touched wound
up turning to shit. Except with the guys he fell in with at the
end, at least for a while. He made some real money with them."

"How do you know?"

"He told me, and he flashed it around. And then he stopped
hanging out as much, like he was too big for me and the other
guys. I told him that it pissed me off, and he said that it didn't
matter, that one day he would suddenly disappear."

Miranda does something with his face and voice, somewhere between a frown and a snicker. "He disappeared all right,
but I don't think that's what he had in mind."

"Was he concerned the cops might be on to him?"

"Now that I think of it, yeah. Near the end he said that
some cop was pressuring him. But he thought he could handle
it. George was confident that way."

"Did he ever mention anything about wanting to start a
company and needing financing?" I ask that because Jacob
Richardson, the R that was apparently dining with Hafner the
night Avery was killed, has a company that funds start-ups.

"Not to me. George wasn't the company-starting type."

"Can you think of any reason that George would have been a threat to national security?"

"You mean the country?"

"Yes, Billy. The country."

"Are we talking about the same George? No way. He thought he was big-time, but he was as small-time as I am."

IN A WAY, GETTING QUESTIONED ABOUT THE AVERY KILLING WAS POTEN-tially good news for Vince Petri.

The situation obviously contained some risk for him, but it was nothing that he was particularly worried about. He was a suspect back during the original investigation, but the cops couldn't pin it on him then and gave up trying fairly quickly. There was no reason to think they could do any better now.

Nothing had changed since then. Nobody had seen him make the hit, and his alibi witnesses were still intact.

In fact, the two guys with the dog weren't even cops, or at least Vince didn't think so. They didn't act like cops, and they didn't identify themselves that way. He didn't know what their interest was, but he was looking forward to making them regret the other night. The next time they wouldn't see him coming.

But the positive development was that it gave him a reason

to reconnect with the man he knew only as Curtis. He still had no idea who Curtis was, or even if that was his real name.

But he knew that Curtis's money was good.

And he knew Curtis was no one to mess with.

But Vince saw himself as no one to mess with either. Money was his driving force, and since he was getting low on it, he called Curtis on the number Vince had only used once, almost two years ago.

Curtis surprised him by answering the phone with a simple statement: "I hear you got a visitor."

"How did you know that?" When Curtis didn't seem to consider that a question worth answering, Vince added, "I don't even know their names."

"Corey Douglas. He used to be a cop."

"Sounds about right. What do you want me to do about it? Can we make another arrangement?"

"We can meet and talk about it. It's time for a second assignment."

That was exactly what Petri wanted to hear. He was going to get back at those guys anyway; it was even better to get paid for it. "Good. Where and when?"

"Tonight. Eleven o'clock. Same as last time."

Vince did not have to ask where Curtis meant; Vince remembered it well. It was an abandoned warehouse in Garfield. He hadn't been there in two years, but he assumed that nothing had changed.

"I'll be there. Same money as last time." Vince did not frame it as a question. He knew he wasn't in a position to dictate terms, but his style was to be aggressive. He could take less and it would still be lucrative.

"We'll talk about that," Curtis said.

Vince showed up on time. The warehouse was as it was

before, but dark and seemingly empty. He did not see a car or any other indication that Curtis or anyone else was already there. But the door was open, so he went inside to wait.

The only light inside was from moonlight entering through the window, so it was almost impossible to see anything. But suddenly that changed; the inside of the building lit up with a piercingly bright light that temporarily blinded him.

Long before Vince's eyes had time to adjust, the bullet entered his forehead, followed by two others in his chest.

"Nice to see you again, Vince," Curtis said. "It's been a while." Then, "But don't worry; we'll take care of Douglas without your help."

WHEN CONDUCTING AN INVESTIGATION, NOT BEING A COP HAS ITS DIS- advantages.

One of them is getting people to talk. As a cop, I could always threaten that if the subject didn't talk where we were, I could instead force him or her to come down to the station.

The threat was often empty, but nevertheless usually worked. People seemed to find the prospect of facing cops where we had the home-field advantage intimidating.

I can't use that anymore, even though we are employed by the police department. Sometimes I imply that I'm still a cop without actually saying it, and the subject just buys it. But I don't want to do that with Jacob Richardson, the R that had dinner with George Hafner. I want the full weight of the department behind me.

To that end, I asked Pete Stanton to clear the way for

me, and he had one of his lieutenants contact Richardson. He told Richardson that I was employed by the department, and that I would be questioning him as part of a murder investigation.

Apparently, no threat to conduct the interview at the precinct was necessary. Richardson was fine with taking the meeting, and it was set up at his Paramus office this morning, which is why I am here.

The office is in a strip mall near where Route 4 meets Route 17. Only six cars are parked in the lot, and none are near the entrance to JR Capital, Richardson's company.

The door is open, and I enter a small lobby with an empty reception desk. The lights are on, which is the only indication that the place might not be totally deserted.

I call out, "Hello?," which is the most clever thing I can come up with under the circumstances. It doesn't work, so I try it again, and then again.

"Detective Douglas?"

I look over and see that a man has appeared, apparently through a side door. I'd say he's in his early forties, dressed casually in khaki pants and a polo shirt.

"That's me."

He walks toward me, smiling. "I'm sorry, my assistant has the week off." He holds out his hand to shake, and I oblige. "Jacob Richardson."

"Nice to meet you, Mr. Richardson."

"Friends call me Jake."

I nod. "If we become friends, I'll make the adjustment."

If he's put off by that, he doesn't show it. The smile is still on his face as he invites me back into his office.

The office is what you would expect in a small strip mall.

He sits behind the desk, and I take the only chair across from it. If three of us were meeting, one would have to stand.

"So the lieutenant said that this has to do with a murder investigation? I have to admit I'm curious."

I don't feel in the mood to satisfy his curiosity, so instead I say, "Tell me about George Hafner."

He has a blank expression on his face. "I'm afraid I'm not familiar with the name. Who is he?"

"You had dinner with him at Marcella's restaurant almost two years ago."

"I just don't remember that at all, but I have dinner with a lot of people, and almost always at Marcella's. It's often for business. Can you give me more information about this man?"

"The way these interviews tend to work is that I ask the questions and you provide the information."

"I understand, but I'm afraid that if that's the case, then the result of this interview is going to be unsatisfactory for you, because I do not remember Mr. . . . . Hafner, is it?"

"Yes. Do you often have dinner for two with people you don't know?"

"If it will help, I'll check my calendar from back then, which is at home. But I sometimes meet with people who are interested in financing for a venture they are planning. On occasion, when no other time is convenient, we might have dinner. It's possible that is why I met with Mr. Hafner; it is certainly a restaurant that is a favorite of mine. I have an ownership interest in it.

"But I do not remember this person, and I definitely did not ultimately do business with him."

The only progress I've made so far is removing the fake smile from his face. "What companies do you do business with?"

"That is private information which I cannot imagine is relevant to your investigation."

"I can have it subpoenaed if necessary."

His tone turns cold; I'm pissing him off. "That would certainly be necessary, and if I'm ordered to do so, I will comply.

"Look, Detective, I don't remember Mr. Hafner. It's possible that we could have had dinner and I have forgotten the event. But it's not possible that I murdered him and forgot that. That would stick out in my mind. Now, if there is nothing else . . ."

"There is plenty else. But that will be for another day."

I get up and leave. I liked nothing about Jacob Richardson, and I trusted him even less. I don't believe that this is an active business; there is no indication of that at all. Yet he obviously has a source of money: he takes a limo to dinner at a restaurant he owns in Paterson.

I also don't believe that he wouldn't keep his business calendars at his office, and I doubt he forgets someone he had dinner with, though that is certainly possible.

But I have absolutely no reason to believe that just because he had dinner with a person in Paterson, who was murdered three weeks later in Queens, that he was involved in the killing of either Hafner or Danny Avery.

Of course, there is one other thing. I did not tell him that George Hafner was the murder victim; for all Richardson should have known Hafner could have been a suspect, a witness, or related in some other way. But he sarcastically denied murdering him. It could be that he just jumped to a conclusion, or he could have some independent knowledge that Hafner was a victim.

But I am keeping an open mind.

I call Sam and ask him to do a cyber-examination of Richardson and his business. It's a long shot, but I can't get over that the night Danny Avery was murdered, he was likely watching a restaurant in which a patron was himself murdered three weeks later.

Obviously, the fact that Avery might have been watching Hafner doesn't prove that Hafner's dinner companion has anything to do with this. But it's a thread we will pull on until it reveals something or demonstrates that nothing is there.

DANI IS HOME WHEN I GET BACK; SHE'S SITTING ON THE COUCH WITH Simon watching television.

Simon doesn't care what kind of show they are watching as long as he is getting petted, so I think that Dani prefers him to me as a TV companion. But she does seem happy to see me.

I am definitely happy to see her. "How was the event?"

"Level three."

"Great."

Dani's assessment of an event has three levels to it. Level one is a disaster, meaning something has gone terribly wrong. The flame under hot-food dishes caused a fire, or a windstorm knocked over the outdoor tent, or the waitstaff got into a brawl with the guests.

Level two is fine . . . nothing special but nothing went wrong. The majority of events are level two.

Level three is outstanding; everyone was thrilled and the

event went off like clockwork. The Miami event was apparently in this category, and I'm happy for Dani. Her job has a lot of pressure; she's responsible for everything, even those things that she has little or no control over.

"How's the case going?"

"Level two. No disasters yet, but no definite progress."

"Sorry to hear that."

"I think we need to get away."

"I was just away. What's going on?"

"I thought we'd go to a hotel in upstate New York for a day or so."

"I'm missing something here. You want to come clean?"

"If I have to. It's related to the case." I go tell her about Jimmy staying at that hotel, and how it seems completely out of character.

"Why didn't you tell me that in the first place?"

"I wasn't planning to hide it, it's just that deception is my natural default position."

"We need to work on that."

I go to the computer to make a reservation at the Demarest Hotel in Chapin Falls, New York. First I ask Google how far away it is; it's a four-hour drive. Not too bad.

What's bad is the price. The hotel looks beautiful and is clearly highly rated. But the room rate, for the most basic room, is $600 a night. Pete Stanton is going to go batshit when he sees it on our expense reports. I make the reservation, making a mental note not to order the most expensive bottle of wine at dinner.

Dani looks over my shoulder as I'm on the hotel website. "Wow. We're going there?"

"Nothing but the best for my woman. And get this: pets are allowed."

"I should hope so."

We go into the den. Mercifully, Dani has a book she wants to finish, so I watch a college football game with the sound off, so as not to disturb her. I don't mind; there are few football announcers that I regret not listening to.

It's deep into the second half when the phone rings and I see that the caller ID says PATERSON POLICE. Could Pete Stanton be working late and spying on me and knows I'm going to an expensive hotel and charging him? No chance.

I answer it and the caller identifies himself as Donnie Griffith, the lieutenant who worked the Avery case and told me about Vince Petri.

"You're shaking things up, I see," Griffith says. "I sure don't want to get on your wrong side."

"What are you talking about?"

"Vince Petri."

"What about him? Marcus and I talked to him the other night. He's a real charmer."

"You haven't been watching the news?"

"No . . . football. Why?"

"Somebody did more than talk to him. A bunch of kids playing in an abandoned warehouse in Garfield found his body. He was shot three times, including once in the middle of his forehead. Those kids have some therapy in their future."

"I had no idea. But I'm going to miss his wit."

"You think you triggered something?"

"I can't imagine how. We had a nice chat, we smacked him and a few friends around, and we drove him home. It was all quite civilized, and we were affable as always."

"Sounds like a pleasant evening."

I get off the call. Even though my telling Griffith that I don't know how Petri's death could be related to our talking to him was true, I believe that it was very much related. Otherwise it would be a huge coincidence, and I don't even believe in small coincidences.

One positive in my mind about Petri's death is that it makes it more likely that he killed Danny Avery, and thus he was himself killed to keep him quiet. That means that it's likely that Petri's comment that Danny was "dirty" was self-serving bullshit. I'm glad about that; I hate the rare times when cops go to the other side.

I tell Dani about the conversation with Griffith, and she asks if I have any idea who could have killed Petri.

"No. But until I find out that it had nothing to do with us, I'm going to assume that it did."

"Which means you could be next."

"One never knows. But I can't imagine why."

"Is it possible that Petri came at Marcus to get revenge for the other night, and Marcus killed him?" Dani has come to know Marcus quite well since she and I have been together.

I shake my head. "No chance. Marcus wouldn't have shot him; he would have beaten him to death."

"Good old Marcus."

"WE'RE NOT GOING TO DO ANY HEAVY INVESTIGATING," I SAY. "MAYBE A few questions."

"Four hours by car would be a long way to go just for Dietrich to have a liaison," Dani says. "Unless the woman lived up there."

"There is not a chance in hell that's what he was doing. When Jimmy wanted to get away and relax, he went out on his boat. But I have to admit I have no idea why he was going to the hotel."

"Does Petri getting killed mean anything to your case?" Dani has developed an interest in what I do, but more as a game of strategy. When it turns violent, she turns off, probably because she is a normal human being.

I also like the mental challenge; I see it as a puzzle that has to be put together. But while I rarely verbalize it to Dani, I take the danger and violence in stride and occasionally relish them. It's necessary and I don't shy away from it.

There is some Marcus in me.

"I would think Petri is directly tied into it, but I don't know how yet," I say. "I want to see if the cops come up with anything, but I have my doubts. Laurie has been in contact with them, and from what she's heard so far, they think it was a professional job, which is code that means they don't have anything to go on yet."

"But what does he have to do with Jimmy Dietrich?"

"Nothing yet. Petri was my main suspect in the Danny Avery murder, and much more so now. But we've been operating under the theory that the three killings were related. If we're wrong about that, then Petri has nothing to do with our little outing today."

We settle in for the rest of the ride. You can learn things about people on a long car ride, and this one is no exception. Dani reveals herself to be a compulsive radio-button presser. She simply cannot stand for one moment when a song that meets with her approval isn't playing, so she constantly jumps from station to station.

She plays the radio buttons like they are a keyboard; she is the FM version of Rachmaninoff.

As we near the hotel, we are on a pleasant country road, one lane in each direction. It's the kind of place where I'd expect to see small stands along the side selling freshly grown local blueberries or some other produce. If I see a kale stand, I'll pick some up for Julie Simonson.

We make a left at a sign for the Demarest, and even though I think we're on the hotel grounds, we can't see it from here. Then we see it from a distance, as we pass a turnoff with a sign that says SERVICE AND DELIVERIES. The road seems to lead to the back of the hotel.

"That's the peasant entrance," I say. "It's not for us; we're important, six-hundred-dollars-a-night big shots."

Dani smiles. "We're not going to have to interact with peasants, are we?"

"No chance. Stick with me, kid."

We continue along to the front. If there is a nicer setting for a hotel than the Demarest's, then I don't know where it is. Maybe Maui or Tahiti, but maybe not. This is obviously not on a beach, but it is nestled in the woods along a spectacular lake, with a long driveway leading to a building so perfect for the area that it looks like it might have grown here naturally, rather than having been built.

The hotel is eight stories high, and nine steps lead up to the front entrance. I know these things instantly because I am a compulsive counter; I can't help myself.

For example, Dani recently dragged me to see a high school production of *Guys and Dolls* that her niece was starring in. In a scene near the end Sky Masterson rolls a pair of dice against the other people present, for $1,000 each. It's when he sings "Luck Be a Lady."

I would bet that I was the only person in the audience who counted the number of people onstage with him. If you're scoring at home, old Sky was risking $19,000.

We get out of the car, and in moments the valet and a bellman descend on us. We head up the stairs and into the lobby, not surprisingly classy and expensively furnished. Even Simon looks impressed.

"Elegant," Dani says.

"So this is what six hundred dollars a night buys."

"Corey, of all your cases, I think this is my favorite."

We check in, and I notice a sign saying that in a few weeks the hotel will be closed for two weeks for renovations. They say it's to ensure a more luxurious experience for the guests, and maybe it is. Or maybe it's off-season and they want an excuse to lay off their staff for two weeks.

When the desk clerk sees Simon, he gives us a dog water bowl and packet of biscuits along with our room key. And in a particularly nice touch, he asks Simon's name and puts it on the room reservation as well.

We are on the fourth floor, which takes us longer to get to than it should on the slow elevator. It's the first demerit for the hotel, but I am willing to overlook it because the elevator has a velvet bench to sit on.

I'm surprised Dani is even willing to take the elevator; she views them as pure evil. To her, stairs are the perfect way to ascend to heights, while at the same time ensuring fitness.

But she gives in this time, maybe because we have a suitcase. I notice that the elevator only goes as high as the sixth floor, though I had counted eight when we pulled up. Maybe particularly high-class suites are up there with their own elevator. I'd try to get one, but I have a feeling Pete is going to be pissed off enough at the $600 room.

We have a couple of hours before dinner, so Dani goes to check out the gym and spa. I could use a nap, but instead I take a look around the hotel.

The grounds are what one would expect: a beautiful pool area and three clay tennis courts, all of which are unused because summer is long over.

Not many guests are here; as nice as it is, probably only a limited number of people will pay this kind of money to hang out in the middle of nowhere at this time of year. For me, money is no object, as long as it's Pete's money.

Unfortunately, I don't see any neon signs explaining why Jimmy Dietrich was here. Since I'm a detective, I decide to do some detecting and I head back inside.

I go over to the bar, unoccupied except for the bartender, washing glasses. I have no idea who dirtied the glasses in the first place, but someone must have.

"Good afternoon, Mr. Douglas."

"How did you know my name?"

He shrugs. "Part of the job. What will it be?"

This doesn't seem like a beer kind of place, but I order a Bud Light, and one appears with an iced glass.

"Welcome. We don't get many first timers; most of our guests are repeaters."

I don't ask him how he knows I'm here for the first time; I assume that's another "part of the job." But I can't pass up this opportunity, and I take out a photo of Jimmy Dietrich and show it to him.

"Was he one of the repeaters?"

"Mr. Seifert? Sure, I remember him. Straight Scotch. Haven't seen him in quite a while."

This response jars me. For one thing, Jimmy's drink of choice was straight Scotch, so it makes it likely that the bartender does remember Jimmy.

But more significant is that Jimmy used the name Seifert. Captain Ron Seifert was Jimmy's boss in the department, and the fact that Jimmy was using a fake name shows he was concealing his real identity. That could be consistent with his having an affair, but I don't think there's a chance that's why he did it.

"Was he with anyone when he was here?"

"I don't really like talking about the guests, you understand, but I'll make this one exception. I never saw him with anyone. He seemed to just sit over in that corner, drink his Scotch, and people watch. Seemed like a nice enough guy."

"By the way, the hotel has eight floors, but the elevator only goes up to six. Why is that?"

"There's another elevator on the other side of the lobby." The bartender points. "Over there."

"What's up there? Special fancy suites?"

He shakes his head. "No. There are some apartments that people own, but as a vacation place; they're not here all year. And on the seventh floor there's a medical office, accounting, that kind of stuff."

"Is there a doctor on full-time?"

"No, a nurse. You ask a lot of questions." He doesn't say it in a negative way, but with a smile. If he's being guarded, he's hiding it well.

Out in the main area of the lobby, some arriving guests are being greeted by a tall guy, maybe forty years old. Handshakes all around.

"One more question. Who is that?"

"That's Mr. Barkley."

"Oops . . . one more. Is he the manager or something?"

The bartender smiles. "Or something. He owns the place."

I thank him, finish my beer, and go back to the room. We have an early dinner reservation, and Dani is already showered and getting dressed when I get back. I do the same, and we head for the restaurant.

When we arrive, three parties are on line ahead of us waiting to be seated. I'm struck that the maître d' calls everyone by name. There's "Good evening, Mr. Simons," "Nice seeing you again, Dr. Powers," and "Welcome back, Mr. Daniels."

When it's our turn, he calls me by name and we're led to

our table. The prices on the menu will be enough to make Pete gag, but the food is terrific. I don't quite finish my steak, so I can bring a piece back to the room for Simon. I do finish the chocolate soufflé dessert; it's so good I'm tempted to order a second one, but I exercise restraint.

We leave early in the morning. It's been an extremely pleasant trip; I need to work on more investigations like this.

Unfortunately, I only learned a few things. Jimmy did stay at the hotel, probably alone. He used a fake name, and the chocolate soufflés are outstanding.

"THE POLICE DO NOT HAVE ANYTHING TO GO ON IN THE PETRI MURDER," Laurie says.

She's been checking in with them for updates. She doesn't relish the job because she knows they have a great deal to do on their own cases without being bothered with ours. But she is so much better at getting cooperation than I am that the job has necessarily fallen to her.

She continues, "They still think it's a professional hit, and I don't think anyone is staying up late worrying about it. Based on the life Petri led, the prevailing view is that he got what he deserved."

Laurie and I have gotten together at her house this morning to compare notes. "The question is whether our conversation with him the other night somehow triggered things," I say.

"Marcus has talked to two of the guys who were with him that night. One of them was a guy who had run away from you two when the action began, and the other apparently wasn't bright enough to do so and wound up unconscious."

"I remember it well. What did he learn?"

"They claimed to have no idea who killed Petri, or whether it had anything to do with the other night. They didn't want to say any more, but Marcus can be fairly persuasive."

"I'm aware of that."

"They said that Petri had an employer that they couldn't identify, but that paid really well. Petri would never talk about it, but they believe that this employer had to be the source of his money."

"Did he kill Danny Avery?"

"They swore they didn't know, but they've always thought it was possible. That was back around the time that Petri started flaunting his money."

"So with us reopening the case, maybe Petri's employers wanted to make sure that he wouldn't talk, either intentionally or by mistake. So they made sure that couldn't happen."

"If that is true, then you and Marcus could be targets as well."

"I have already been so advised."

"Dani is a smart woman," Laurie points out accurately.

She asks me about our trip to the Demarest Hotel, and I tell her about everything except the chocolate soufflé. When I'm finished, I say, "Whatever Jimmy was working on, it brought him to that hotel. He wasn't vacationing there, and he wasn't having an affair."

"You're probably right, but we don't know that for sure."

"I do. The bartender said he was always alone. But the fake name locks it in for me. Let's say he was having an affair, with Susan Avery or anyone else. Why use a different name? Was some suspicious husband going to check the records of the Demarest Hotel, four hours from civilization?"

"True. And we know from Susan Avery's credit card records that she was home during at least two of Jimmy's trips."

"We need to pay more attention to Susan. I don't know about you, but I've been focused on Danny and Jimmy. I've just semi-assumed that Susan was collateral damage. Maybe she was a real target, maybe not."

"I think probably not," Laurie says. "But you're right, we shouldn't eliminate the possibility."

"I've got the name of her closest friend. I'm going to have a talk with her."

"Today?"

I shake my head. "Tomorrow."

"Good, because we have a full day ahead of us. Sam delivered all the phone and credit card records for Danny and Susan Avery, and Jimmy Dietrich. I only glanced at them so far, but there's some potentially interesting stuff in there."

We start going through it, and Laurie is right, not so much about Danny Avery, but more about Jimmy Dietrich. In addition to the trips to the Demarest Hotel, he placed phone calls to three cities that I did not know he had a connection to. They were Chicago, Philadelphia, and Detroit.

Notably, he also flew to Chicago, coming home the next day. He might have flown to see whoever it was he had called the day earlier, and I will look into that.

Much of this needs further follow-up by Sam; certain calls and credit card usages could be either meaningful or benign. We'll tell Sam which things to look more deeply into, and that will tell us what might be worth our time, or not.

One other thing jumps out at me. The plastic surgeon that

Susan Avery consulted and paid money to was named Dr. Jonathon Powers.

When we were on line waiting to go into dinner at the Demarest Hotel, the maître d' greeted one of the guests as Dr. Powers. I have no idea if that is the same guy; Powers is not a terribly unusual name, but it's not Smith either.

If the Dr. Powers at dinner is the Dr. Powers that Susan Avery paid, that would qualify in my mind as an interesting development in our investigation.

Even though I don't have any idea what it would mean.

RILEY DEVANEY SAYS THAT SHE AND SUSAN AVERY WERE BEST FRIENDS.

"I certainly think she felt the same way. We were literally friends since day one: our mothers gave birth in the same hospital just twelve hours apart." Riley smiles. "I was born first. I used to tell her she needed to respect her elders."

I'm at Riley's house in Saddle Brook. For years a Marcal Paper plant nearby dominated this working-class neighborhood, but it burned down. Now the landscape consists of a few tall hotels off I-80, just a twenty-minute drive from the George Washington Bridge.

She seemed anxious to talk to me when I called her. I don't think it's because she feels she has anything significant to say; I think it's more that she just wants to renew some kind of connection to her old friend.

"I'm sure she took that advice to heart," I say.

Riley laughs. "Not quite." Then, "I miss her every day. We finished each other's sentences."

"Did you finish each other's sentences much in the month or so before she died?"

"We talked some, though not as much as usual. She had just lost Danny a few months before, so I was giving her some space. She knew I was here for whatever she might have needed."

"Did you know anything about her relationship with Jimmy Dietrich?"

"Not really. One day I went over to her house, and he was just leaving. There was an awkwardness to it; almost as if there was some secret that I walked in on."

"Could they have been having an affair?"

Her response is instantaneous and firm: "Absolutely not."

"Why are you so adamant about that?"

"Look, I'm not saying that Susan would never have dated again. And certainly with her husband gone she would not have been doing anything wrong by doing so.

"But the pain of losing Danny was way too fresh; there is no chance she would have been open to any kind of relationship at that point. And with an older man like that? Not Susan. It is just not possible."

"Did you know she called a surgeon a few weeks before she died?"

Riley seems surprised. "Really? Why did she do that?"

I avoid the question. "So you're not aware of any health issues she might have had?"

"No. She would have told me; we told each other everything."

"Would she ever have considered plastic surgery?"

"No. She hated the idea. She mocked the celebrities who had way too much work done."

"So when you first heard the news, that she had been found dead of gunshot wounds on that boat, what was your first reaction?"

"You mean beyond horrified and upset?"

"Yes. What did you think might have happened? Your gut reaction."

"I thought it had something to do with Danny. I still do."

"What do you mean?"

"She was devastated by Danny's death, but the circumstances made it even worse. She became obsessed and haunted by the fact that his killer was out there, living a life of freedom. The way he snuck up on Danny, like a coward, and shot him . . . she couldn't stand that."

"So you think she did something to provoke the killer?"

"I can't say that I think that because I don't know what it could have been. But you asked for my first reaction, and that was it."

"But she never talked specifics of what she might have been doing to help find Danny's killer?"

"No, not to me. I know that she kept calling the detectives on the case, asking for updates and information. But she would often complain that they weren't doing enough, that they weren't getting anywhere.

"I wanted to say something to ease her pain, but there was nothing I could say. That pain was legitimate; she lost her husband."

"Was she distraught enough to possibly have committed suicide?"

I expect an immediate no, but that's not what I get.

"I don't think so. It doesn't fit at all with the Susan I knew. But I've never gone through what she went through. I've never been in the pain she was in. So could someone snap? Could

Susan have snapped? I couldn't rule it out, but I'd be shocked if it were the case."

For a moment I think she is going to cry, but instead she just adds in a soft voice, "That would be so sad. This whole thing is so sad."

WHEN I CALLED KATHY LINDER IN CHICAGO, I WASN'T SURE WHAT TO tell her.

I knew that Jimmy had called her three weeks before he died, and I knew he flew out to Chicago the day after he called her. But I couldn't be 100 percent certain that he had gone to see her.

So I played it straight. I told her that I knew she had been in contact with Jimmy Dietrich eighteen months ago, and that I wanted to talk to her about that contact.

She seemed anxious to talk, but she had some questions, including "Do you have any information about Roger?" Since I had not the vaguest notion who Roger was, I avoided that and other questions by saying that it would be best if we talked in person.

She was fine with that, which is why I took a 6:00 A.M. flight and landed at O'Hare a half hour ago. My hope is to get a five o'clock flight back this afternoon, but that will depend on my conversation with Kathy Linder.

I grab an Uber at the airport and head out to Highland Park, the Chicago suburb where she lives. It's supposed to be a twenty-five-minute drive, but the traffic turns it into forty-five.

Kathy Linder's house is not spectacular, but close. It's in an obviously exclusive neighborhood of beautiful homes, and hers is above average even for this area. It's set way in from the street, with a large, perfectly manicured lawn, and professionally maintained landscaping nearer to the house.

She comes out to greet me when the car pulls up and, after confirming that I am Detective Douglas, invites me in. She seems so anxious to talk that I think if I move too slowly, she will grab me by the neck and drag me.

We sit in the den, where she has coffee and some kind of cookies already on the table in front of the couch. "I'm very anxious to hear what you have to say," she begins.

"I think I should start off by managing expectations. I am here to gather information, not to dispense it. If I have anything helpful to you, I'll certainly share it. But for now, I'm conducting an investigation that on some level you may be involved in. If that leads to something helpful for you, that would be excellent for both of us."

She looks disappointed. "I understand. Ask your questions."

"What did Jimmy Dietrich come to speak with you about?"

"Roger."

"Who is Roger?"

She seem momentarily taken aback. "I see you really aren't going to be very informative."

I feel the need to change the momentum here, so I say, "Well, here's something you might not know. Jimmy Dietrich, the man who came to see you, was murdered three weeks after he was here."

She gasps and her hand goes to her face. "Oh, no . . . how awful. But what could that have to do with Roger?"

"And Roger is . . ."

"My husband. Or he was my husband; I divorced him in absentia."

"I would appreciate your telling me the story; I'm most interested in what you discussed with Mr. Dietrich."

"Well, he was asking questions about Roger, so I'll start at the beginning, or actually at the end. Amazingly, considering how it upended my life, there isn't that much to tell."

She pauses and seems to take a deep breath to steel herself. I don't say anything; I find it best not to interrupt someone offering information, unless the spigot seems about to turn off.

"Roger and I were married for four and a half years. He worked for an investment bank; he was a senior vice president. If he was unhappy, beyond the normal aggravations of business and life, he effectively concealed it. Or maybe I was just oblivious.

"Then one day he left. No conversation, no phone call, no note, nothing. I came home one day and his clothing was gone, along with his personal papers. I literally had no idea what to make of it; it just came as a sudden and total shock.

"Even though it should have been obvious that I had been abandoned, I called friends of his and members of his extended family to ask what they knew. All of them claimed to be totally unaware of what could have happened; they professed to be as bewildered as I was. I had a better relationship with some of them than he did, so I believe they were telling me the truth.

"I called the police and made a report. I felt a little ridiculous doing so because it was obvious that they considered it a husband bailing out of an unhappy marriage. And down deep I thought they were right; I guess my ego made it hard to come to terms with being left like that and admit it.

"But he wasn't just leaving me; the people at his company also were completely taken by surprise. So Roger wasn't just leaving a marriage; people do that all the time, albeit perhaps not as suddenly or dramatically. He was also leaving a lucrative and successful career that he had spent years creating. I knew that to Roger work and money were extraordinarily important.

"And then I started to get some worrisome phone calls, tentative at first and then more direct. Audits were revealing Roger had been embezzling money from the bank. I never got all the details, but it involved some kind of wire-transfer fraud. We are talking about huge amounts of money . . . many millions. And he had taken it with him.

"I wound up in major litigation, but when the facts came out, my excellent lawyers carried the day. There was no money of Roger's left for them to recover." She smiles. "Yes, I know you're thinking that this woman is not living in poverty, and I'm not. I came into the marriage with a great deal of family money, and thankfully it remained with me."

She seems finished, so I ask, "And you haven't heard from Roger since?"

"No. Two people have reported seeing him in Copenhagen, and maybe that's true and maybe it isn't. The truth is that, while I'm curious, make that *anxious,* to know where he is and what happened to him, it doesn't really affect my life anymore.

"I've moved on; we're not going to get back together and ride off into the sunset. He is a thief, and he chose great wealth, even greater than we already had, over me. It didn't do my ego any good, but I've come to accept it."

"So what did Mr. Dietrich say when he was here?"

"Well, he asked a lot of questions, and I told him everything I told you. Then he said that he hoped to be able to answer my questions very soon, that he was putting it all together. I never heard from him again, and now I know why. The poor man . . .

"I have to say that even though there is so much about Roger that I did not know, and even though he is obviously a thief, I cannot believe he would have been involved in any kind of murder. He hated violence; he couldn't even watch it in movies."

"That's good to know."

"And you'll let me know if you learn the truth? I said that I moved on, and to a great degree I have, but closure would be nice."

"Ms. Linder, I will do my best to provide it. I can promise you that."

DANI AND I LIKE TO PICK EACH OTHER UP AT AIRPORTS.

Maybe *like* is too strong a word to use; picking each other up is just something that we started doing and has become something we reflexively do.

I wind up being the pick-up-er more than the pick-up-ee because Dani travels for work a lot. But when I'm not there to greet her, like the other day when she returned from Miami, I feel guilty.

This evening it's her turn to be there when I land at Newark Airport, coming back from Chicago. She doesn't come into the terminal because Simon is with her. Once I'm in the car, I ask, "Did you cook dinner?"

"No, I didn't think that would be fair to you."

"Excellent." Dani has a clear understanding of her abilities, or lack of same, in the kitchen. I shudder to think what a disaster it would be if she thought she could cook and expected me to eat the slop she would put on my plate. Of course, I am even more inept in the kitchen than she is.

So we stop at a diner with outdoor seating for a quick meal. It's cold out, but Simon is not allowed inside, and we're sure as hell not going to leave him in the car.

While we're eating, I tell her about my conversation with Kathy Linder. I find it helpful to bounce things off Dani; she's a good listener and asks helpful questions that often provide a fresh perspective.

When I'm finished, she asks, "Why would Jimmy Dietrich be interested in an embezzler from Chicago?"

"I don't know. But that may not even be the important question. If Jimmy was investigating Danny Avery's murder, as we think he must have been, then the real question is 'Why would Danny Avery have been interested in an embezzler from Chicago?' Jimmy was just following Danny's tracks."

"Do you have an answer to that one?"

I shake my head. "Not a clue."

"So you now think you've connected Avery to George Hafner and maybe Roger Linder. You know that Homeland Security was interested in Hafner, right?"

"Right."

"So maybe Linder, or the bank he worked for, was financing someone or something that was a threat to national security? Is that possible?"

"Possible. Makes as much sense as anything else I've come up with."

"And maybe Jacob Richardson, who had dinner with Hafner and who finances start-ups, was contributing money to the bad guys as well?"

"Also possible."

She smiles. "Let me know when you figure it out."

We leave the restaurant and head home.

As we drive toward the front of my house, I see a small bulb lit on my mailbox. "Drive past the house."

"Why?"

"Just do it. Keep driving; don't slow down. We'll pull up on the next street and I'll tell you what's going on."

Dani does as she's told, and when she eventually pulls over, she says, with obvious concern, "What is it, Corey?"

"I think someone is in our house."

"How do you know that?"

"That's not important right now; we can talk about it later. Here's what you need to do. I want you to make three phone calls, and the order in which you make them is very important."

Once I'm sure that Dani has memorized exactly what I've told her, I take Simon and start walking back toward our house. I take a detour onto the street behind the house, so we can go through a neighbor's backyard into my backyard.

It's dark back here, so I don't think we can be seen. Besides, if there really is someone in the house, they will be focused on the front door, which is how we usually enter.

Once I see the back door, all doubt is erased. The door is closed, but it's clear that the lock has been broken. This is how the person got in, and whether he knows it or not, this is definitely how he is going to go out.

Now all I can do is wait. I look at my watch; if Dani does exactly as I told her, she will be calling in four and a half minutes. I move close to the door, so that I will be able to hear.

Sure enough, right on time, I hear the phone ringing. After five rings, the machine picks up, as programmed. I can hear Dani's voice leaving a message.

"We know from our cameras that you're in the house. I just

called the police. Have a nice night, asshole." I'm sure she was nervous about making the call, but it doesn't come through in her voice at all. She sounds angry, determined, confident, and fully in charge.

If the guy in the house doesn't panic, he will wonder why the voice on the phone is tipping him off that the police are coming. The smarter move for the homeowner to make would be to keep him unawares until the cops can arrive and capture him.

If he does panic and is not thinking clearly, then that "mistake" by Dani will not occur to him. But either way, his reaction will be the same; having lost the chance to surprise us, he will want to get the hell out of the house. He'll leave through the back door, the way he came in. That way he won't be seen, and if the cops show up quickly, he won't run into them.

But the back door is where Simon and I are waiting.

I'm looking forward to meeting him, and I think Simon is actually salivating at the prospect.

About ten seconds later the door opens, and the intruder comes out. He doesn't see us in the darkness at first, so I say, "Freeze, asshole!"

But he doesn't freeze; he runs. I could shoot him, but I hate shooting people in the back, even if they deserve it. So instead I say, "Simon, get!"

And Simon gets; Simon is one of the best "getters" you will ever run into. He makes up the distance between us and the intruder in a few seconds and brings him down by chomping onto his leg. The guy screams in pain.

I run toward them, and as the intruder turns over, I see that he has pulled out a gun. I don't know if he's planning to shoot Simon or me, but that doesn't matter. Both of those choices are unacceptable.

My own gun is already out and pointed, so I shoot him twice, both bullets hitting him right in the chest where his intact heart used to be.

I go over and shine my phone flashlight at him, so I can get a look at his face. If I've ever seen him before, I don't remember it. And it's bad form to ask a guy you just shot and killed if you've ever met before.

But either way, I'm not planning to apologize, nor am I feeling any regret. I don't like shooting slimeballs like this in the back, but the front I'm fine with.

LAURIE AND MARCUS ARRIVE AT THE SAME TIME, ABOUT FIVE MINUTES after the situation has been resolved.

There's nothing for them to do; they were going to be back-ups in case Simon and I ran into difficulty.

We didn't.

Five minutes after that the police arrive in force. Dani obviously made the phone calls in the exact manner and on the exact timing I had given her. Four squad cars appear, followed by two more. Pete Stanton is a passenger in one of them.

The intruder, not surprisingly, hasn't moved and will never again move. Once one of the officers determines that he is deceased, he calls the medical examiner and a forensics team.

Pete takes in the scene. "Let's go have a talk, shall we? By the way, who fired the shots?"

"That would be me."

He just nods, and we all start to follow him toward the

house. Dani arrives, and I motion for her to join us. Pete gives me a look, so I say, "She was an integral part of what went down here. And watch out, there will be prints on that door. Let's go around through the front."

So we make quite the parade . . . Pete, me, Laurie, Marcus, Dani, and Simon. In a normal situation, Pete would want to question the shooter, me, alone. But this is not a normal case, so he's not objecting to their presence.

Once inside, we go into the kitchen, the least likely place for the intruder to have left any prints. But if he was here, and if he sampled any of our leftovers, then he really did suffer tonight.

"Why don't you just start at the beginning?" Pete says. "And try to keep the bullshit to a minimum."

I relate accurately everything that went on from the time we first drove up to the house. As I'm telling the story, I'm doing mental checks if there's anything I should conceal or be deceptive about, but I don't come up with anything, so I tell it straight.

Dani nods along as I'm mentioning her, and when I finish, she says, "I made the phone calls just like Corey asked."

"Nicely done," I say. Then, "Wait until you guys hear the phone message she left; she even scared the shit out of me, and I'm the one who dictated it."

Pete doesn't seem amused. "Why didn't you tell her to call nine one one first?"

"Well, to tell you the truth, I thought we might have been mistaken. Maybe there was no one in the house at all; I didn't want to waste anyone's time."

"Yeah, right," Pete says scornfully. "What made you think anyone was there?"

"There's a motion detector in the house; Sam Willis helped

me install it a while back. It turns on a small light on the mail-box out front. I almost never use it, but because I had reason to believe someone might be after me, I used it tonight."

"Why was someone after you?"

I turn to Laurie. "Might be time for an update."

She nods her agreement. "Pete, we believe we know who killed Danny Avery, but we might not ever be able to prove it. The shooter was most likely Vince Petri. He's the scumbag who got killed in Garfield the other night. He was a close associate of the guy Danny killed in that domestic violence incident."

"The very one," I say. "Marcus and I had a conversation with him the other night. It was rather unpleasant."

Pete turns to Marcus. "Did you kill him? Wait a minute, don't answer that."

"Marcus didn't do it," I say. "But someone apparently found out about our conversation with him and might have been concerned that we were getting close to the truth, and that maybe Petri couldn't be trusted not to talk. At least, that's our theory."

"If Petri killed Danny to avenge his friend's death, then why would someone have killed Petri to keep it quiet?" Pete asks.

"Good question," Laurie says. "We haven't figured that part out yet. But just like someone considered Petri a threat, they obviously think the same about Corey. And I'd bet that's the same reason they killed Jimmy Dietrich and Susan Avery."

Pete frowns. "Let me know when you figure it out." Then, "Who is the guy that they are probably loading into the coro-ner's van right now?"

"We'll be anxious to find that out ourselves," I say. "None of us have ever seen him before."

Pete calls in two of his detectives, and I go into the den with them so they can take down my official statement. I'm glad they are not making me do this down at the precinct; I just want to get it over with and go to sleep.

It's hard to believe that my early flight to Chicago was this morning; it feels like a week ago.

DANI AND I WERE SO WIPED OUT WE WENT RIGHT TO BED, BUT WE BOTH knew that "the talk" was going to happen this morning.

She kicks it off with "That was incredibly frightening last night."

"I know, and I'm sorry. But you were amazing."

"I should have said it was incredibly frightening for me. You weren't frightened at all."

I shrug. "I was concerned."

She shakes her head. "You ate it up with a spoon."

"It's what I do. And in this case, I could not help myself. This guy was in our home, waiting to kill us. I could not let him stay in there a minute longer than I had to. I'm sorry you had to experience it, but it was the best way to handle it."

This is not the first time Dani has been dragged into something like this. Last time it happened, she was in great personal danger and barely escaped with her life.

"Did you want to kill him?"

"No, but not because of any concern for his well-being. He had a gun and was going to shoot either me or Simon. But I wanted to find out who sent him. Now we will have to find out another way."

She gets quiet, so I add, "Look, I don't want you to experience things like this. You shouldn't have to be a part of this world. I just wish I knew of a way to accomplish that."

She doesn't say anything for at least a minute . . . a really long minute. Then, "I want to be with you, which means I have to take the good with the scary. It's who you are and I have to accept all of it, just like you have to accept all the junk that I bring to the table. Like my cooking."

"That's different. Your cooking can't kill me. Well, maybe it can, but it would be my own fault for eating it. And my cooking makes you look like Julia Child."

She laughs, and the tension is broken . . . for the time being.

"You really were amazing, especially with the phone message you left. You handled it perfectly."

"Thank you."

"What was going through your mind?"

She thinks for a moment. "I wanted the son of a bitch out of our home."

What I don't tell Dani is that if one guy came after me, another one might follow. It's unlikely that killing one guy we've never seen before took care of the problem. We'll have that conversation tonight, when we both get home from work.

For now, Simon and I head to Laurie's to assess where we are and figure out where we are going. As soon as I get there, Laurie tackles the issue head-on.

"We need to set up a schedule of some kind. When you're going to be out while Dani's home, Marcus is going to have to watch your house. There is too much chance that they are going to take another shot at you."

"Agreed. Dani goes to Vegas on Wednesday for a few days to handle a convention, so that's well-timed and will make it easier on Marcus. Maybe we can wrap this up before she gets back."

"Seems unlikely."

I nod. "I know. Wishful thinking."

I bring Laurie up-to-date on my trip to Chicago and conversation with Kathy Linder. Not surprisingly, she also doesn't understand why Jimmy Dietrich would have flown out there to talk to her; there just does not seem a logical connection between her disappeared investment-banker husband and Danny Avery's death.

Sam calls with some new information. "I've looked into Jacob Richardson's business as much as I can. I don't want to say it's a shell company; I can't go that far. But the start-ups he's funding are few and far between, and he's putting very little money into them."

"I'm not terribly surprised," I say. "The office just did not seem like an active place of business."

"It isn't."

"He said that if he had dinner with Hafner, then it was probably Hafner asking for seed money."

"Well, he didn't get any, that's for sure. Very few people have gotten money out of Richardson. He hasn't started up very many start-ups."

"Can you get a list of those companies that did?"

"I have it already. I'll send it over to you. But there's only three of them; something called Mannion Partners, Winter Life, and FGI."

"What does FGI stand for?"

"I have no idea."

"No, that would be IHNI."

It was a bad joke, Sam didn't get it, so we move on. Sam has one other piece of news for us, and that is to say there is no record of a Dr. Powers at the Demarest Hotel; he certainly didn't register there or pay for anything with a credit card.

"Could you have gotten the name wrong?" Laurie asks me when we get off the phone.

"I don't think so, but anything's possible. I had no reason to remember it at the time."

"Did you get a good look at him?"

"Just the back of his head. It was not memorable. I'll ask Dani if she saw him, but I doubt that she did."

I call Caroline Dietrich back and ask her if she has any idea why Jimmy would have gone to Chicago.

"While we were together?" she asks.

"No, about three weeks before he died."

"I'm sorry, Corey, he never mentioned it to me, so I really don't know."

"What about the Demarest Hotel in upstate New York?"

"Never heard of it."

I run through some of the other names that have come up so far in this investigation, and Caroline draws a blank on all of them.

"Caroline, did Jimmy keep any kind of a journal? Or any papers that might be related to his work? You said you hadn't cleaned out his office yet; is that still the case?"

"I'm afraid so; I'm slowly getting up the strength, but it's a process. I suppose there could be papers in there."

"Could I look around? I won't mess anything up."

"If you want to, sure."

I tell her that I'll be by either later today or tomorrow. It's a long shot, especially since during the last weeks of his life Jimmy was not living there and so would not have accumulated any papers. But it's not like we have any better ideas.

Laurie and I spend some time planning our next steps, but we're interrupted by a call from Pete Stanton. Both Laurie and I get on the phone to hear what he has to say.

"Corey, the guy you shot last night was named Joey Wingate. Better known as Joey 'Icepick' Wingate."

"Let me guess . . . he wasn't a college professor. Or a librarian."

"Definitely not. I take it you're not familiar with him?"

I look at Laurie, who shakes her head. "Neither of us are, Pete. Who is he?"

"He's a hired gun, or hired icepick if you will, out of Philadelphia. He was currently a prime suspect in the murder of one Wilson Dozier. There's been an arrest warrant out on him for a long time, but he hasn't shown up anywhere until now."

"Who was Wilson Dozier?"

"He owned some kind of manufacturing company with a partner. The theory is that Wingate was paid handsomely by someone for removing Mr. Dozier from the scene. Apparently, a number of people were in a position to profit from Dozier's death."

"So someone here brings in a wanted hit man from Philadelphia to try and kill me? Is there that much of a scarcity of local talent?"

"I wish there was."

AT THIS POINT, IAN SOLIS PROBABLY KNOWS MORE ABOUT AMERICA'S power grids than anyone else in the world.

He knows that there are five major interconnection grids in North America. Two of those are much larger than the others; they are called the Eastern and Western Interconnections.

He knows that were either of those to fail for any significant length of time, the results would be catastrophic. People in those areas would not just be without lights, they would also have no water, no gas, no heat, no refrigeration . . . the list goes on and on.

He knows that even without major chaos as a result of a grid failure, people would unquestionably die in large numbers.

He knows that the grids are girded and protected against the possibility of cyberattacks, and until now those safeguards have been effective. The many efforts to evade them have all been detected and thwarted.

Until now.

The Eastern Interconnection has been invaded by a silent enemy. The defenses have been penetrated, and the attack can be launched at any time.

The experts assigned to protect the grid will be helpless . . . when they find out what is going on.

Which will be soon.

Ian Solis knows that.

I'M RETHINKING MY VIEW OF DANNY AVERY'S CONNECTION TO GEORGE Hafner.

I still strongly believe that the link between them was and is there; I don't think it's a coincidence that Avery and Hafner were both murdered within three weeks.

They somehow presented a danger to people whose style is to eliminate danger ruthlessly and violently. Vince Petri's demise proves that, and I believe so does that of Jimmy Dietrich and Susan Avery. And if I need any more proof, I can just glance out my bedroom window and look at the bloodstains in my backyard.

But Danny was a New Jersey cop. He was not an FBI agent; his scope was local. George Hafner lived in Queens, with no obvious connection to this area. Somehow Danny and Hafner became united in death, but I don't think that the situation began with the two of them. Hafner could not have been Danny's initial focus . . . or at least I don't yet see how.

But Jacob Richardson was a different story. He lived in New Jersey, had an office in nearby Paramus, and owned and dined frequently in a Paterson restaurant. One of those dinners, on the night that Danny Avery died, was with George Hafner.

So I've revised my point of view. I think it far more likely that Danny's investigation started with Richardson and expanded to include George Hafner. That is especially true because Sam thinks that Richardson's business of supposedly investing in start-ups is essentially a front.

A front for what? Beats the hell out of me. It can't be money laundering because Sam says the company spends and takes in little money.

But with limited investigative routes open to us, I decide it's time to put some pressure on Jacob Richardson. Vince Petri showed clearly that our adversaries respond to pressure, and if we increase it, maybe someone will make a mistake.

So it's time to rattle Jacob Richardson's cage a bit more. Unfortunately, our cage-rattling toolbox is not exactly filled to overflowing. In a perfect world we would get a search warrant and turn his business and home upside down, but we have no probable cause of anything.

A judge would laugh at whatever cop would have the guts to bring in the request.

Enter Sam Willis, who as always answers the phone on the first ring with "Talk to me."

"Sam, I know you hacked into Richardson's business computer system."

"*Hacked* is an ugly word."

"Sorry."

"I prefer *cyber-entered.*"

"Okay. My question is, Would Richardson have known that you cyber-entered?"

"Of course not."

"Is it possible to go back in, to both his business and personal stuff, and make it obvious that someone was in there searching?"

"Sure. But it's beneath my dignity as a cyber-entry expert."

"Sometimes in this business we have to check our dignity at the door. Can you let him know someone was searching, but conceal the fact that it was you?"

"Absolutely."

"Once you do it, can you monitor his phone? I want to know who he calls."

"On it."

"Good. Go for it. But make totally sure that it can't be traced back to you. We are dealing with unpleasant people."

"I hear you."

"Also, see what you can find out about Roger Linder. He's an investment banker from Chicago who embezzled a lot of money and then took off about two years ago. Jimmy Dietrich called his wife and flew out to talk to her before he died."

"I'm on it."

"Thanks. And, Sam, I can't emphasize enough how important it is that you keep your fingerprints off of everything. We don't know who is who yet, so assume the worst about everybody."

I get off the call with the unpleasant feeling that we are floundering. I don't really expect someone like Jacob Richardson to panic over this, but there's no downside to trying.

Somewhere there is a connecting link between George Hafner

and Jacob Richardson and Roger Linder and Vince Petri and "Icepick" Wingate and unnamed guests of the Demarest Hotel.

It's a link that Danny Avery was probing, and Jimmy Dietrich after that.

It got both of them killed.

CAROLINE DIETRICH IS WAITING ON THE PORCH WHEN SIMON AND I pull up.

She seems a little nervous and after greeting me says, "Are you sure you want to do this?"

"I do. Are you still okay with it?"

She smiles. "I guess better you than me. Come on."

Simon and I follow her into the house and to the base of the stairs.

"You remember which room it is, right?"

"Of course I do."

"The cleaning person has gone in there occasionally to vacuum and dust, but please excuse the condition you find it in." Then, "Come on, Simon. I've got some biscuits in the kitchen."

They walk away; Simon doesn't even look back at me. He would follow anyone who used the word *biscuits*. When it comes to food, loyalty is not his strong point.

I head up the stairs to Jimmy's office. We used to play gin in there and drink. I'd have beer and he'd have Scotch, straight, no ice. I hadn't been nervous about coming here today, but I have to admit that it's starting to feel a little weird.

The door is closed but unlocked, so I take a deep breath, open it, and go in. It's in better shape than I expected, and definitely better than when Jimmy was alive and using it. He was not the neatest guy in the world.

Not that much is in here. He had always kept some clothing in the closet, mostly shirts and jackets, but they're gone. Jimmy had moved out a while before his death, so he obviously took most of that kind of stuff with him.

A filing cabinet is in the closet, so I start to go through that. I don't find anything of interest, at least not to our case. It's mostly tax and insurance stuff, and things related to the house. His passport is in here, and some other personal things.

I go over to his desk, which has three drawers. I start at the bottom and feel my first jolt of emotion. In there is a baseball, and I remember the exact moment he got it. We had gone with a few other guys to a Mets game, and Jimmy caught a foul ball hit by David Wright.

If you have ever been to a baseball game or seen a baseball game or lived on planet Earth, then you know how exciting it is to catch a foul ball. The same ball you could buy for ten bucks is like gold when it lands in your hands at a game. I think it was the happiest I had ever seen Jimmy.

But it doesn't really help with the case, and the second drawer is no different. Jimmy's badge is in there; I guess he somehow avoided turning it in. There are also some papers, none of which hold any significance to me, and probably not to him.

The third drawer seems different. At the very top of some

papers are two newspaper clippings. They have apparently been printed off the internet from the *San Francisco Chronicle*, and they relate to an arrest warrant out for Ian Solis, a resident of San Pedro, California.

The details are sketchy, but Solis was wanted on suspicion of cyber-terrorism activities. He was an employee of a tech firm in Silicon Valley, but apparently took off before he could be arrested. The FBI had established a tip line for information as to his whereabouts.

I search through the rest of the drawer, but there is nothing else of interest to me, and nothing more about Solis. I fold the articles and put them in my pocket.

I leave the room and head back downstairs. Caroline and her fiancé are sitting on the sofa with Simon between them; he is thereby receiving four hands' worth of petting.

"Sorry to interrupt, Simon," I say. "You've been a huge help."

Caroline smiles. "He seems comfortable. Did you find what you need?"

"Not really. But thanks for letting me try." I don't see any reason to tell Caroline about the articles. It would just provoke questions that I can't answer, and maybe some anxiety in her as well.

I thank her and we leave. As soon as I get in the car, I call Sam. I hate burdening him, but his talents are unique to our group.

"Sam, there's a guy named Ian Solis, and he's—"

"Sure, I know him."

"You know him personally?"

"No, I mean I know about him. He's a legend among hackers."

"I thought you didn't like the word *hack*."

"For him it fits. The guy is a terrorist. He gives the profession a bad name."

"Was he ever arrested?"

"No, I don't think so. If I remember correctly, he just disappeared. I haven't heard about him in a while."

"I need to know everything there is to learn about him."

"I'm on it. Tomorrow morning okay?"

"See you then."

"SUSAN AVERY MIGHT HAVE MADE THE DIFFERENCE," LAURIE SAYS, "BUT I can't find anyone who knows anything."

We're at her house the next morning, waiting for Sam to come over with whatever information he has come up with. Laurie is frustrated because she's been interviewing friends of Susan Avery's, none of whom can enlighten us as to what Susan was doing in those last weeks of her life. All they are able to tell Laurie is that Susan seemed disconnected from them and consumed by something . . . but they don't know what that something was.

"What do you mean by 'difference'?" I ask.

"Well, we have all these pieces, and we can't seem to make them fit together. Jimmy Dietrich had the same pieces, but he obviously had an idea what was going on. He was on a clear path."

"What does that have to do with Susan Avery?"

"She might have known things, through Danny, maybe documents that she found among his things. She was working with Jimmy to do what Danny died trying to do. And didn't her friend say that she was obsessed with finding out who did it?"

I nod. "She apparently felt the police were botching the investigation. Danny had felt the department sandbagged him because of the domestic violence shooting, so that probably played into her attitude as well. She might have felt the same resentment."

"Maybe she found someone in Jimmy who she could trust, and who shared her desire to solve the case. So she told him what she knew and gave him what she had."

"Makes sense," I say. "Caroline said that Jimmy was a mentor to Danny, so I'm sure he must have known Susan well. But it's possible we'll never know Susan's role in this. And regardless, it doesn't help us now. We have to fit the pieces together without any kind of road map."

Sam comes over, and after he scouts through the refrigerator for any available sustenance, we go into the den to hear what he has to say.

"Okay, I went into Jacob Richardson's cyber world, and I left prints that would make Bigfoot proud."

"He'll see them for sure?"

"Yes."

"If it was me, would I see them?" I ask.

"Probably not, but you are unique when it comes to tech expertise. Or lack of same."

"I can send emails; doesn't that count for anything?" Then, "Has he made any phone calls in the time since you cyber-entered his world?"

"I don't know. I only did it this morning. I'll check it when I get back and keep an eye on it."

"Okay. Where are we on Ian Solis?"

"Well, I can't say I have much more information than I had beyond what I already knew. I've copied some more stuff off the internet, but it's mostly media reports."

"Why don't you tell us what you know," Laurie suggests.

"Okay. Ian Solis is famous among people who do what he does, which is invade computer networks."

"That's what you do too, right, Sam?" she asks.

"Yes, but I do it for a good cause. Solis quite apparently doesn't. I don't know what the Feds nailed him on, but it apparently was some kind of terrorist activity. I assume they thwarted it because the world hasn't blown up."

"So he made a mistake?" I ask.

"The word in the 'community' is that he did make a mistake, but it had nothing to do with his online work. Apparently he confided something to a friend or coworker, and they ratted him out."

"Anything else the community is saying?"

Sam nods. "Yeah. They think he stole some crypto currency on the way out the door. Nobody knows how much, and like I say, it's just what people believe. I can't confirm it."

"What makes him so good?" I ask. "The ability to break in anywhere?"

"That's part of it, but there's a lot of people that can do that, including yours truly. The real trick is to do it without leaving a trace, so no one can track it back to you. You always read that the Russians are good at it, but we know exactly who they are, even what building they're working out of. We can't get to them because they're in Russia, but they always leave cyber finger-prints. Solis is light-years ahead of that."

"And he's still out there?" Laurie asks.

"Apparently so. In a case like this, I would think they'd

make a big deal out of catching him if they did, as a deterrent to others. But no one has said a word. And he's a guy that could cover his tracks very effectively."

"What about Roger Linder?"

"That's an interesting case. I printed out what I have on him, but it's basically as you described it. He took off on his wife and job and is wanted for embezzling a lot of money. There is speculation that he got away with upwards of twenty-five million."

"And no trace of him?"

"Not that I can find, and I've looked. He's off the grid; not an easy thing to do. He may be out of the country."

I nod. "His wife told me that there had been a couple of reports of sightings in Copenhagen. Any chance you see a connection between Solis and Linder?"

"None, although I haven't really looked for that. The arrest warrant on Solis went out months before Linder embezzled that money."

"I'm going to call Tony Alvarez," I say. "See what he has to say about Solis."

"You think he'll give you any information?" Laurie asks.

"Maybe we can trade."

"But we don't know anything."

I smile. "I didn't say it would be a fair trade."

TONY ALVAREZ IS AN ASSISTANT DIRECTOR AT HOMELAND SECURITY. Andy Carpenter introduced him to me a while back, and we worked together on a previous case.

He's a straight shooter in a job that basically requires him not to shoot straight with guys like me, so our dealings back then were awkward and filled with deception, but ultimately fruitful for both of us.

I call his office and they say they will take a message. If memory serves, Alvarez is not the most responsive guy in the world, so I leave my number and tell his assistant that it's a matter of life and death.

He calls back within five minutes. "Life and death? You played the life-and-death card?" Obviously he didn't buy it, but called back anyway.

"I have a tendency toward the dramatic. But in this case it could actually be true."

"You scared the shit out of my assistant."

"Good. Your staff needs some toughening up. The security of our homeland is at stake."

"You want to get to the point? Because my hanging up is imminent."

"I want to talk to you about Ian Solis."

"And who might that be?" He sounds like he really is not familiar with the name, which is not necessarily a surprise to me. He's clear across the country from where Solis disappeared more than two years ago, and the Homeland Security guys have a lot on their plate.

"He might be someone you're after."

"I'll look into it and call you back."

"Good. And when you talk to whoever you are going to talk to, throw the name George Hafner into the mix."

He hangs up without so much as a good-bye . . . rude.

While waiting for him to call back, I try to formulate a plan for what I'll do next. Unfortunately, my options are limited or nonexistent, depending on one's level of optimism.

Basically we're trying to retrace Jimmy Dietrich's steps, while figuring out why he took them. We know he was interested enough in Roger Linder to fly out to Chicago. We also know he had an interest in Ian Solis, though just printing two newspaper articles shows something less of a commitment than a plane flight.

But we've followed up as much as we can on Linder, and we'll see if anything comes from contacting Homeland Security on Solis.

Then there is the memorable "Icepick" Wingate, the wanted killer out of Philadelphia who invaded my house and tried to kill me. Why would the same people who employed local talent like Vince Petri to kill Danny Avery bring someone in from Philadelphia to deal with me?

Maybe I should feel flattered; maybe the Douglas legend does not know state boundaries. But I am going to look into it as much as I can.

One area that feels intriguing but underexplored is the trips that Jimmy made to the Demarest Hotel. I have no doubt that they are related to the case he was working, and I am just as positive that case was Danny Avery's murder.

Jimmy wasn't there on a whim, nor was he vacationing. He must have been following someone there. I have no idea who that could be. There was the Dr. Powers that I was behind on the dinner line; he's a possibility because Susan Avery called and paid money to a Dr. Powers.

But he didn't show up on the guest list, nor did he pay for anything at the hotel by credit card. It's also possible that I heard the name wrong; I had no reason to be listening carefully. I was focused on what Pete would say when he saw on the expense report that he was paying for a twenty-two-dollar shrimp cocktail.

Sam has provided us with the guest lists at the hotel for the two months before Jimmy's death, so I start to pore through them. I'm hoping to find a name that was there the same three times that Jimmy was there; I'll even take two.

Unfortunately, as has increasingly been the case, I come up empty. No name appears more than once when Jimmy was at the hotel; if he was following someone, they're not among the registered guests.

What I don't have, but would like, is a list of the people who own the apartments on the seventh and eight floors that the bartender spoke about. They could have been there each time that Jimmy was; they wouldn't show up on the guest registry.

I call Sam and ask him if he can come up with the names. I

know we've been overloading poor Sam, but he doesn't seem to mind. He seems to relish it.

I have no idea how crimes were ever solved before advancements like computers and DNA. That's why Jack the Ripper probably lived out his days drinking gin and tonics near the Royal Box at Wimbledon.

As soon as I get off the phone with Sam, Tony Alvarez calls me back. "Amazingly enough, you seem to have struck a nerve."

"That was my plan."

"You're going to meet with Special Agent Oliver Baron at three o'clock this afternoon."

"That doesn't give me time to get my hair done."

"You'll manage."

THE ANXIETY THAT JACOB RICHARDSON HAD FELT ALMOST TWO YEARS ago had returned. He hadn't felt it since then, other than through an occasional flash of memory.

But now he was unsettled. That Corey Douglas guy, and his people, were putting pressure on him. First they confronted him directly, and he thought he had defused the situation. But he's discovered that they have been intensifying their investigation into his life.

He thought he could withstand scrutiny; after all, that was the entire purpose behind everything he had done in the first place, to be a convincing front. But there was always the chance that a mistake was made, one that could potentially leave him vulnerable.

He reported the new developments, as he was supposed to, but no one seemed concerned. They seemed to already know all about it, as if what he was telling them was old news.

They sounded confident and told him not to worry, that it was all being handled. It eased his mind somewhat, but not nearly all the way.

He was still worried.

That worry was magnified by a factor of a thousand when Curtis showed up at his house the next night. Curtis always made him nervous; Curtis had from day one. Now they were past day eight hundred, but Curtis's effect on him had not changed.

What made this situation far more frightening was that Curtis just appeared in the house. Richardson did not know how he got in; suddenly Curtis was just standing in the den and saying, "Hello, Jacob."

Curtis had a smile on his face, but his smile never included any warmth or humor. It conveyed menace; it always had.

"How did you get in?"

"Not important. I'm here to talk about your problem with the detective."

"I was told not to worry about it."

"That was correct. Douglas is the least of your worries."

"What do you mean?"

"I'm afraid you have to disappear again."

"No. There has to be another way. I won't do it."

"Of course you will. This isn't a request; you are not being asked for your point of view, or your agreement. You understand that, don't you? You know that was the arrangement all along."

"I know, but there has to be another way."

"I'm afraid there isn't. But I have to tell you that this time it will be different."

"What do you mean?" The words caught in Richardson's throat when he realized that Curtis suddenly had a gun in his hand.

"I mean this time you will be gone for good. And no one will miss you." Curtis smiled again. "That's the beauty of it."

LAURIE SUGGESTED THAT I BRING ANDY CARPENTER TO MY MEETING WITH Special Agent Oliver Baron, and I agreed for three reasons.

For one thing, meetings like this are delicate, and it's important to be careful about what is said. As a lawyer, Andy can see any cliffs that I might be barreling toward and stop me in midflight. It's probably not necessary, but it can't hurt.

For another, Andy has had some experience with Baron; they've dealt with each other on a previous case, which according to Andy ended well. Of course, Andy's idea of ending well might be different from Baron's.

Lastly, Laurie negotiated Andy's hourly rate down to zero, which seemed quite reasonable.

Agent Baron is based in the Bureau's Newark office, but he said that he was going to be in this area this afternoon, so we're meeting in Andy's office on Van Houten Street in Paterson.

It's basically a dump above a fruit stand. I've never understood why Andy hasn't upgraded; he can certainly afford it. It might be some kind of nostalgia thing, or maybe he likes ripe peaches.

Baron is on time, and when he sees Andy, he says, "Oh, shit. You again?" Andy has a way of annoying people; and Baron has clearly experienced it firsthand.

"Stop," Andy says. "I promised myself I wouldn't cry."

Baron turns to me. "You're Douglas?"

"I am."

"Why did you bring him?"

"He's my attorney."

"And a damn good one," Andy says.

Baron frowns and turns back to me. "What do you know about Ian Solis?"

"I was about to ask you the same question."

"That's not how this is going to work."

Andy stands up. "Thus ends this meeting. Thanks for coming, Agent Baron. You can pick up a cantaloupe downstairs on your way out. On us."

Baron doesn't stand up. He tells Andy, "You are adding absolutely nothing to this conversation."

"You're not the first person to tell me that. But it hurts every time."

It might be time for me to take over. "We are conducting a murder investigation, retracing the steps that the victim, who was a retired police officer, took in the weeks before he died. The names Ian Solis and George Hafner have come up. In the case of Solis, we need to know whatever you can tell us about him."

"And in return?"

"In return we tell you what we've learned so far and keep you updated on our investigation. I would describe that as a no-downside situation for both of us."

He thinks for a moment, as if deciding. It's nonsense; he has been told well beforehand what he can say and what he can't. "Deal."

"Good. So you were about to tell us about Ian Solis."

"Much of this is public knowledge. He's a domestic terrorist; it runs in the family. His father is still serving time, and you could say it soured the son on the government, and society in general. He was planning to take down an electric grid. Actually, that may not be entirely accurate. He was planning to have the capacity to take down the grid if the government did not pay what I am sure would be a very substantial blackmail."

"How did you uncover all of this?"

"He shared what he was doing with someone he thought was sympathetic to his efforts." That confirms rumors that Sam heard. "We caught a break; Solis is a genius and his plan would otherwise have not been uncovered until it was too late."

"And you have no idea where he is now?"

"We believe he is overseas, probably Russia. The problem is that he is just as dangerous to us there as here."

"How so?"

"It's an interconnected world, and it's not like Solis needs colleagues around him. You know how the media talks about people like Tim McVeigh and guys like the Unabomber as being lone wolves? Well in cyberland . . . that's where the lone wolves truly are. The cliché is true that a guy living in his mother's basement can impact the world."

"But you don't know what his target is this time?"

"We don't even know if he has a target, but you can be sure that whatever he is doing it will not be beneficial to society. This guy is not teaching Computer Programming 101 at Moscow University. He is a true radical, and he has no conscience."

"Did Solis walk away with a lot of money in Bitcoin?" That

was another of the rumors that Sam picked up through the "community."

Baron reacts. "How did you know that?"

"We heard a rumor, that's all."

He nods. "Twelve million dollars. That can buy him a lot of borscht in Russia."

"Why were you interested in George Hafner?"

"Who told you we were?"

I'm certainly not going to throw Lieutenant Sewald, the Queens cop who told me that Homeland Security pulled Hafner's file, under the bus. So I say, "I'm afraid I'm going to have to invoke informant-detective privilege on this one."

Baron frowns; he doesn't care for my answer, but he can do nothing about it. "There was contact between Hafner and Solis; we didn't learn about it until Hafner was already dead. We think Hafner may have made Solis a fake passport; that was one of Hafner's specialties."

"So who would have killed Hafner?"

"That we don't know, but whoever it was is the nexus between Solis and Hafner." Then, "I believe you have the floor."

"So I do." I lay out what we have learned so far. Actually, *learned* is the wrong word, because we haven't learned anything.

But we have accumulated a lot of pieces in a so-far-unassembled puzzle, and I detail all of them to Baron. We have a mutual interest here. I don't care who puts that puzzle together; if the FBI can solve the murders of Jimmy Dietrich and Susan Avery, I'm all for it.

Also, if Ian Solis is truly the danger that Homeland Security obviously thinks he is, then I also am all for doing anything I can to put him away.

Baron certainly seems interested in everything I have to

say. Rather than take notes, he records my voice on his cell phone, with my permission. He claims to have no knowledge whatsoever about Roger Linder or Jacob Richardson, and I have no reason to doubt what he is saying.

When we're finally done, we agree to keep each other updated, though I doubt his people will go along with that. In any event, there are handshakes all around and a promise to keep in touch.

"Do I still get the cantaloupe?" Baron asks.

Andy nods. "Absolutely. Just mention my name downstairs."

IT'S TIME TO RATTLE ANOTHER CAGE, THE ONE THAT HOUSES DR. JONA-thon Powers.

I had Laurie make the call because she can be far more persuasive than me. She said her husband was in agony with a hand injury and needed to be seen right away. Playing the role of husband for this performance is Corey Douglas.

Dr. Powers apparently heads up a group called Bergen County Surgical Associates, but Laurie said that she wanted her husband to see Powers, that he came highly recommended. No other surgeon would do.

So here I am. I just finished the six-page health-history questionnaire that the woman behind the desk gave me, lying all the way through it. I almost put down that I was pregnant, but I thought that might make them suspicious.

I wait in the dreaded waiting room for forty-five minutes, which in this case is not unreasonable. They had told Laurie that they were fitting me in, and that there would likely be a wait. They repeated that to me when I signed in, so I have nothing to complain about, especially since the magazines are relatively new.

I'm finally brought to an examining room, where I wait another ten minutes until Dr. Powers comes in. I can't tell if he's the guy I saw at the Demarest Hotel because I had only seen the back of that person's head. If Powers had walked into this examining room backward, I might have a better idea.

He smiles. "Good afternoon, I'm Dr. Powers."

I return the smile. "And I'm here under false pretenses."

"I don't understand. You don't have a hand injury? What does that mean?"

"My name is Corey Douglas, and I am a private investigator conducting a murder investigation on behalf of the Paterson Police Department. You can call the head of Homicide if you need confirmation of that fact."

"What does this have to do with me?" His face reflects both surprise and concern. I would doubt that very many of his patients come in talking about murder, at least not before he bills them.

"A woman came to see you about a year and a half ago; her name is Susan Avery."

"Okay . . . did I perform surgery on her? I cannot place the name. I must say this is very irregular."

"Murders are like that. But, no, you did not operate on her."

"Then why is her coming to see me important?"

"She was murdered soon after being here."

He seems taken aback, which could obviously be a fake. "Oh, I'm sorry to hear that. That's terrible. But I am still unclear as to what it is you want from me. Am I some kind of suspect? Do I need a lawyer? This is ridiculous."

"Have you ever been to the Demarest Hotel in Chapin Falls, New York?"

"Yes." He says it without hesitation. "I was there just recently for dinner. Why do you ask?"

I ignore his question. "Was that the only time?"

"No, I've had dinner there before."

"Did you stay there as a guest any of those times?"

"No, I have a friend who lives in the area. I thought you said this woman was killed years ago."

"Who paid for dinner?" I ask, ignoring him.

"That same friend. Look, you really need to tell me what this has to do with a person who was killed that long ago."

"No, actually I don't need to do that at all. All I need to tell you is what I have already told you; that I am investigating a murder. Your name has come up in connection with the case."

He frowns. "Look, I am very busy."

"I know. Thanks for fitting me in."

"Do you have any other questions?"

"Not at the moment, but you can be sure I will. You can be very sure of that."

He does not look pleased about that.

I stand up and flex my right hand. "It feels better already. You're a genius."

DANI CANNOT JOIN ME BECAUSE SHE'S STILL IN VEGAS, SO THIS TIME I'M heading to the Demarest Hotel alone.

She wasn't pleased and asked me to bring a chocolate soufflé back for when she gets home, but I have a feeling that one would not survive the four-hour drive back to Paterson. And if it didn't melt, I'd probably eat it on the way.

I also didn't bring Simon with me this time. No sense having him cooped up in a car for eight hours. Instead I drop him off at Laurie's so he can hang out with her dogs. It will also give him a chance to regale Tara with the story of the other night, when he got to chomp on Icepick Wingate's leg.

For lunch I stop at a Burger King about a half hour from the hotel; I'm feeling generous, so I don't even think I'll expense it to Pete and the Paterson PD. This one's on me.

I'm not checking in or making a dinner reservation. I'm here for one purpose: to talk to Steven Barkley, the owner of the place. The bartender pointed him out to me last time; he was welcoming apparently repeat guests as they came into the lobby.

Through the wonder of the cop-to-cop connections that run everywhere, Pete has gotten a local cop to call ahead and clear the way for Barkley to speak to me. I would have preferred to surprise him, but that would have included the risk that he would be out or claim to be too busy to talk to me or just outright refuse.

I tell the reception clerk that I am here to see Mr. Barkley, and moments later he appears. He stops for a moment to greet a guest . . . he seems to know everyone . . . then approaches me. "You must be Mr. Douglas."

I nod. "I must be."

He holds out his hand. "Steven Barkley. We can talk in my office."

I follow him across the lobby to an elevator. It's the one that the bartender told me goes to the seventh and eighth floors. I was hoping to get a look at what was up there, and now it seems like I'm going to.

He waves his key over the control pad and presses number 7, which coincidentally is where the elevator takes us. When we get off, we walk past some offices, which have glass walls allowing them to be seen from the hallway. Not surprisingly, these offices seem to be staffed by office workers.

Barkley sees me staring in. "This is accounting, personnel, and some executive offices for the hotel. Mine is down there."

We walk a little farther and enter an office with the word MANAGER on the door. There is an assistant's desk, but it's empty at the moment. We go into his office, which is modest.

"Are you the manager or owner?"

He smiles. "Guilty as charged. Or maybe that's the wrong phrase to use with a detective. I am both of those things,

although I certainly have investors that participate in ownership. But the Demarest is my baby."

"What's on the eighth floor?"

"Apartments that are fully owned by guests. There are only
four of them, and one is empty and available, if you're interested."

I'm not sure if he's mocking me; I'm sort of sensitive about
stuff like that. But he seems reasonably genuine, so I let it pass.
"Maybe you can show me around after we talk?"

"Happy to. Now, what can I do for you?"

"A couple of years ago, you had a guest here named Jimmy
Dietrich. He used the last name Seifert when he was here."

"He didn't use his real name? Why?"

"He had his reasons. He was investigating a murder and
had no reason to come here other than in service of that investigation."

Barkley looks surprised and concerned, but is smart enough
to let me get to where I'm going.

"We don't yet know for sure why he came here, other than
that it was to surveil one of your guests or a member of your
staff."

"I'm at a bit of a loss for words, which is quite unusual
for me."

"Mr. Dietrich—Mr. Seifert in your records—was himself
murdered shortly after his last visit here."

"I thought I was at a loss for words before, but that is nothing compared to now." Then, "How can I help you?"

"I need to know who he was following."

Barkley pauses a moment, as if to collect myself. "Mr. Douglas, to my knowledge our guests are basically fine, upstanding
people. Having said that, I will candidly tell you that we don't
do a background check on them. No hotel does.

"While I casually know many of them, it is strictly based on their stays here; for the most part I know nothing about what you might call their 'real life.' For example, you stayed here last week, and I did not know you were a detective. We take our guests at face value."

"I understand."

"My employees are a slightly different matter in that we do background checks before we hire them. They may not be rigorous, but we adhere to industry standard. To my knowledge they are fine, honorable people. Certainly I have never heard otherwise."

"I did not expect you to point to someone today and say, 'There's your killer.'"

"Then what did you expect?"

"That you give it some thought, that you go through the guest lists at the time that Mr. Seifert was here, that you tell me of anything that comes to mind. Anything that ever struck you as suspicious or worrisome, regardless of how trivial it might have seemed.

"I would also like you to discuss this with the appropriate employees and see if they have any relevant information or suspicions of their own."

"Very well. I can do all of that. I certainly would want to help in any way I could."

"Thank you. Now, can you show me the eighth floor? I've got a couple of million dollars burning a hole in my pocket."

He smiles. "Well, we can't have that. Come on."

We go out into the hallway and he presses the elevator button. This is my kind of guy, a man who won't even take the stairs up one floor. Dani would be less than thrilled with him.

The door opens, and a guy starts to step off, then realizes he's not on the main floor, mutters, 'Sorry,' and gets back on.

The door closes, and Barkley says, "That's Mr. Walters; he owns one of the apartments upstairs."

We finally take the elevator up to eight. Everything about the hallway, the carpeting, the flowers, the artwork on the walls is richer and classier looking than the seventh floor, or any of those below.

"There are four apartments up here," Barkley says, indicating the four doors spaced along the corridor. "As I said, three are owned, but only Mr. Walters is in town at the moment. They are not their primary residences. The fourth apartment is empty and available."

He walks farther down, and I follow him. The apartment next to the available one has a room service tray on the floor outside it, so that must be the one that Walters owns and is staying in.

Barkley inserts a key into the next door and opens it, motioning for me to enter. I do so and am immediately impressed. It is spectacular, with amazing views. It's only partially furnished, probably just enough to impress prospective buyers.

A large-screen TV in what is probably the den has to be ninety inches. If I lived here, I'd never leave, and I'd have all my meals delivered.

I keep looking around the apartment. There are three bedrooms, a den, a dining room, a living room, and what seems like a game room or office. There is also a kitchen, which has so many modern appliances and conveniences that Dani and I might even be able to successfully cook in it.

Probably not.

There's a door off the kitchen, and as I open it, I say, "What does this lead to?"

"The back hallway and elevator. It's a service entrance."

Now that I've seen everything, I say, "This would work as a starter apartment."

He laughs. "That's how we see it."

"How much is it?"

"A million, seven fifty."

I resist the urge to whistle. "Does that include long-distance calls?"

Another laugh from him. "In Manhattan this would be ten million."

"Yeah, but there you could go downstairs at midnight and get a pizza."

"True."

I thank Barkley and we head back down the elevator. He walks me to the hotel door and promises to call me if he comes up with anything.

I doubt that he will, and I doubt that he'll try. I think his cooperation probably ends here, and he will be happy to see me go and get out of his life.

As I leave, I resist requesting a soufflé to go. I'll stop at the same Burger King on the way home.

There seemed to be nothing suspicious about the Demarest, which makes me suspicious. Barkley couldn't have been more open and helpful, which I never trust in people.

Dogs yes, people no.

TODAY I'M HEADING TO PHILADELPHIA. IT FEELS LIKE I'M IN THE CAR ALL the time; there is not a gas station attendant in the tristate area that doesn't know my first name.

Once again I'm going to be talking to a cop; I didn't talk to this many cops when I was on the force. This time it's a woman, Lieutenant Joy Viola. It was easy to set up this meet and greet since Pete knows her from a case they worked on together about four years ago.

I cleared it with her that it was okay to bring Simon; she said she's a dog lover. The drive should have taken only a little more than two hours, but with New Jersey Turnpike traffic it takes me more than three. Fortunately, I called ahead and Viola said she would still be in her office . . . no problem.

Her office is in Center City, not far from the University of Pennsylvania, one of many schools that I couldn't get into with a crowbar. The precinct looks like every other one in every city in America, which is somehow vaguely comforting.

The desk sergeant does not do a double take or react in any way when he sees Simon. Simon has that police dog look; cops recognize it from a mile away, or from across a reception desk.

In less than a minute we're in Lieutenant Viola's office, and she has a bowl of water and a couple of biscuits waiting for Simon. I get a cup of lukewarm coffee.

"Thanks for seeing me on such short notice."

"Are you kidding? I should be thanking you. Everybody in the precinct should be thanking you. I'm surprised you weren't showered with rose petals when you walked in."

"Why?"

"You killed Joey Wingate. Ding, dong, the witch is dead."

"So you are not a charter member of the Icepick Wingate Fan Club?"

"He was a piece of shit; my only regret is that I didn't shoot him myself."

"Really? He always spoke so highly of you."

She laughs. "So what can I do for you, Mr. Douglas?" It's obviously time to get down to business.

"I obviously have an interest in finding out who hired Wingate to come after me. Not just so I could protect myself from another attempt, but also to help solve a case I'm working on. There are plenty of local people who would be ready and eager to take a shot at me. I need to understand why they went out of state."

"I obviously don't have that answer for you."

"I didn't expect you to. This is an information-gathering mission, so for starters, tell me why you were after him. I know about the arrest warrant for murder, but the details might be helpful."

She nods. "That I can do. He killed a local businessman named Wilson Dozier. Dozier and his partner, Arthur Rucker, made computer chips. They had a factory in King of Prussia, but most of their stuff was made overseas.

"They had a falling-out a while back and had been suing each other over the assets of the company, which were very considerable. It was getting ugly; Rucker was accusing Dozier of stealing from the company. Of course, Dozier denied it.

"One night almost three years ago Dozier's wife received a phone call from him. Her recollection was that he sounded panicked, and he said . . . Wait a minute, let me tell you exactly what she said his words were." Viola takes a piece of paper from a folder on her desk and reads from it: "'Tell David to stop any wire transfers. They made me . . .'"

She puts the paper back. "That was it. He hung up, or someone hung up for him. Either way, he did not get to finish the sentence."

"Who is David?"

"His lawyer."

"And what happened with the wire transfers?"

"Too late to stop them. It was most of Dozier's personal money, and a good portion of the company's. We're talking close to thirty million dollars. It all went to the Caymans to an untraceable account, and the Feds told us that it quickly went on from there. Impossible to trace."

"So the theory is that Wingate, or whoever, forced him to send the wires?"

"That's the theory. In the aftermath, the company wound up declaring bankruptcy."

"Where did Wingate come in? Was he more than just a hired gun?"

"First of all, I should have mentioned that the investigation was a joint effort. We're not sure where the murder was actually committed, but the last time Dozier was seen was getting on a boat in Ocean City. The boat was rented by a fake company. So we worked with the Ocean City police on this."

"The murder happened on a boat?" I don't mention that Jimmy Dietrich and Susan Avery were found dead on a boat, but the fact is not lost on me.

"Yes. Security cameras caught Wingate and Dozier getting on the boat about a half hour after he placed the call to his wife. It went out to the ocean and came back three hours later with only Wingate on it. Dozier was either killed and dumped or just dumped. Either way, he was shark food."

"Are you saying Wingate was the type to pull off a sophisticated wire transfer operation? I don't see it, even though he and I didn't get to chat much."

"No, we don't either. He was a hired hand. Our theory, without evidence that we could use in court, is that Rucker hired him. He unloaded a partner he hated and dissolved a company in trouble, while walking away with a fortune."

"But you could never prove it?"

"Not even close. Rucker has moved on to a new venture, some kind of tech thing. It drives me nuts that he has gotten away with this."

"And Wingate has been out there all this time?"

She nods. "Yup. We assumed that Rucker paid him a fortune and got him out of the country. Then you proved otherwise."

"I assume you brought Rucker in for questioning?"

"Repeatedly. He came in with his lawyer, of course, but answered our questions by denying all knowledge of everything. Pure as the driven snow."

"Do you think he would talk to me?"

"No chance. I could bring him in here, but I'd have to have something new to ask him."

"Do you have tapes of the questioning you did?"

"Sure. You want copies?"

"If you don't mind."

"Are you kidding? You killed Wingate; you could have my firstborn, should I ever have a firstborn."

"Can I pass on the firstborn and get a copy of the tape of them getting on the boat, as well as Wingate getting off when it came back?"

"You sure? My kid would be adorable and smart as a whip."

"I have no doubt of that."

"I'll have to get the interrogation tapes and the boat tapes out of evidence storage, but I'll send copies to you."

"Thanks, you've been incredibly helpful."

"You want a biscuit for the road?"

I accept the biscuit, and Simon and I start the drive back. Of course I call Sam with yet another assignment. "Sam, there's a guy named Arthur Rucker, who is a Philadelphia businessman. He owned a computer chip company that went under.

"I need you to do a deep dive into his finances. How much money he has, where it is, and whether he's moving it around."

"Did you say Arthur Rucker?"

"I did. Why?"

"Arthur Rucker is one of the people who owns an apartment on the eighth floor of the Demarest Hotel."

Holy shit.

Now we're getting someplace.

"THAT HAS TO BE IT," LAURIE SAYS. "RUCKER IS THE FOCAL POINT."

I nod as reluctant a nod as I can manage. "Seems like it."

I think Laurie senses my doubts, so she explains, "Rucker is the prime suspect in a murder case in Philly, a murder that Wingate no doubt got paid to commit. And it was on a boat . . . sound familiar?

"Wingate then came after you, which is why Rucker didn't have to use a local guy. Rucker already trusted him to get the job done. Plus he might not have had local contacts that he trusted.

"Jimmy kept going to the Demarest Hotel for no reason we have been able to figure out, and Rucker has an apartment there. The coincidences would have to be off the chart for this not to all be connected."

"I admit the pieces connect. But it's not held together by logic. Until we understand what's behind everything, I can't fully buy into it."

"What do you mean?"

"It all hinges on one question. What the hell did any of this have to do with Danny Avery? This thing extends to Rucker and Wingate in Philadelphia, Roger Linder in Chicago, Ian Solis in California, George Hafner in Queens, and the Demarest Hotel in upstate New York."

"So?"

I suspect Laurie knows what I'm getting at, but like me, she believes in talking things out. Things become clearer that way.

"So Danny Avery was a Paterson cop sitting in his car on a Paterson street waiting for two people to finish dinner. That got him killed. Why? What do Rucker, Solis, and the rest of them have to do with that? What was Avery onto?

"That is still the key, because Jimmy Dietrich was only picking up Avery's trail. He was finishing the investigation, or at least trying to. That's what got him killed. It's still all about Avery. It's been that way from the beginning."

"But for us, things have changed a lot since the beginning," Laurie says.

It's my turn to ask what she means, so I do.

"We went into this with the goal of solving three cold-case murders," she says. "But it's become bigger than that. The motives behind the murders have moved front and center. It's no longer enough to know who pulled the triggers; we need to know why."

"I agree. And not because we're solving a puzzle. Vince Petri getting killed, and Wingate coming after me, show that whoever we are looking for is still out there, willing to do anything to protect their secret."

"So we start fresh. We start with Avery and look at everything through his eyes. We figure out what he was doing, and why."

I laugh. "You make it sound so easy."

She returns the laugh. "It is. Just let me know when you've figured it out."

I'm about to leave when Sam shows up. He usually calls ahead first, so he either has something interesting to tell us or he's really hungry.

"I brought the Arthur Rucker information. It's all in this folder for you to look at."

"Give us the top line."

"He's as advertised. He came out of his company's bankruptcy smelling like a rose. Plenty of money and a new company that is doing well. But I don't see any unusual dealings. If he has a fortune hidden away, he's not accessing it, as far as I can tell."

"When did he buy the apartment at the Demarest?" I ask.

"Close to three years ago. Paid a million one. He also has a house on Sanibel Island in Florida."

"Thanks, Sam."

"That's not why I came over. I want to talk to you about Jacob Richardson. I've been tracking his calls and his movements as best I can, like you asked."

"What about him?" Laurie asks.

"He's nowhere to be found. No phone calls, no use of his credit cards, hasn't eaten at Marcella's . . . nothing for three days."

"Maybe he's home sick."

"I don't think so. I called his home phone a bunch of times, but got no answer. And that's not the weird part. His cell phone is gone."

"What do you mean 'gone'?"

"It's off the grid. I tracked it the other night. It was in his house, then went on the move. I followed it as it went to north-west Jersey, up near Sussex . . . into a dense, wooded area."

"And then what?" Laurie asks. Sam is dragging it out, but it's safe to say that our interest is piqued.

"Then nothing. It shut off and never came back online. Calling it goes to voice mail. I went to his house and rang the bell; I figured I could make up a story if he answered. But he didn't."

I stand up and start walking toward the door. "Let's go, Sam."

"Where are we going?"

"Jacob Richardson's house."

I'M NOT EXPECTING US TO FIND ANYTHING BEYOND A HOUSE WITH NO one in it, but I have to look.

I firmly believe that Jacob Richardson's going to the North Jersey woods was a one-way trip. A guy who takes a limo to a Paterson restaurant does not pick up one night and go camping in the wilderness, shutting off his phone to eliminate contact with the outside world.

We pull into Richardson's long driveway, which makes our car not visible from the street. We get out and approach the front door. I'm just going to ring the bell; if I'm surprised and Richardson answers it, that won't be a problem. I have plenty of questions I can ask him.

But he doesn't answer it, so we walk around to the side of the house, looking in some windows. There is no sign of life, but it's a two-story house, so there could be someone upstairs.

The carport has two cars in it, and Sam had learned that he

had two cars. That means his drive to the woods was not in his own car. I hadn't expected it to be; I believe he was taken there, almost certainly against his will.

We go back around to the front and I ring the doorbell a few more times. Still no answer, and I turn the knob and see that it is open. It's another sign that Richardson left in an abnormal set of circumstances.

I decide to go in. My reasoning is that I have probable cause to think that a crime has been committed. I couldn't prove it legally, but I'm not going to have to. My belief is good enough for me right now.

I tell Sam to wait in front. "Why?" he asks, clearly unhappy about it.

"I'm about to illegally trespass, which officially embarks me on a life of crime. I'm not dragging you down with me. And this way you can watch and alert me if anyone is coming."

I go inside and call out a few times to give anyone that might be upstairs a chance to come down. I get no answer, and I hadn't expected any.

As I walk around the house, nothing seems out of the ordinary. Certainly it does not seem as if any violence happened here; no furniture seems out of place, and there aren't any obvious bloodstains.

A few plates are in the sink, though that's not proof that Richardson left unplanned. In pre-Dani days, I could go a week without being able to see the bottom of my sink. But a half-filled glass of what seems to be aging beer is on the kitchen table; not something I would ever have done.

I go upstairs and walk through the rooms. In what seems to be Richardson's bedroom, his closet and dresser seem full with clothes. Again, not proof of anything, but certainly it's an indication that he did not go off for a long vacation.

I'm careful not to touch anything, in case this becomes a crime scene. We criminals are smart that way.

I go back downstairs and out the front door.

Sam is there waiting for me. "No sign of him, huh?"

"Nope."

Sam nods. "I told you so."

We head back home. It was what I expected, which is not good news for anyone who might have written Jacob Richardson's life insurance policy.

My belief is that Richardson, like Vince Petri and Joey Wingate before him, has reached the end of his life as a result of contact with Corey Douglas.

I'm at a loss what to do with this information. If I report it to the police, I'd have to leave out some major points, like the fact that Sam has illegally traced Richardson's phone, and I've illegally entered his house.

I decide to sit on the information for a while. Friends and associates of Jacob Richardson's will soon discover that he is missing, if they haven't already. They can report it in.

A day or so is not going to matter to Jacob Richardson.

RICHARDSON'S APPARENT DEMISE MAKES LAURIE'S COMMENT LOOK even smarter.

She said that we need to take a fresh look at the Danny Avery murder, and it was Richardson who was in Marcella's while Avery was waiting outside. If Avery was there to watch Richardson, then finding out why Avery was interested in him is the key to everything. Richardson's death shows that he was right in the middle of whatever the hell this conspiracy is about.

So that's what I'm doing today. I have a copy of the thick file that the cops had on the Avery case, and I'm going to sit on the couch with Simon and pore through it again. I'm also going to drink a couple of beers while doing it, but that shouldn't factor in negatively.

Dani is back from Vegas—I picked her up from the airport last night— but she's out working today, so the house is quiet.

I'm not a big fan of quiet, so I turn on the television for background noise. Then I get to work.

Three hours in, I've gotten nowhere. I'm just reading and rereading reports that I've read and reread before. For all their considerable efforts, the detectives had only partially succeeded in one area, and that was in identifying Vince Petri as a person of interest.

They suspected him, but he had an alibi, so they reluctantly dropped it. They didn't have anywhere near enough to make a case; all they had were their suspicions. I think their hunch was correct, that Petri pulled the trigger.

But my view is they got the motive wrong; they thought Petri was extracting revenge for the death of his so-called friend Frank Gilmore in the domestic violence incident. I don't think it was that at all; I think there was much more to it.

But the cops knew nothing about George Hafner or Jacob Richardson or any of the other things we have uncovered. So obviously there is nothing enlightening about those things in the file; they could not document what they were totally unaware of.

We're aware of all those things, and all those people . . . we're still just baffled by what they mean.

I get to the evidence collection in the Avery case. There is page after page about the spent bullet and shell casing and blood spatter and shooting angle. The forensics people had a field day with it, although they came up with nothing that pointed toward the identity of the killer.

Next up for my reading enjoyment is the cataloged contents of the car that Avery was killed in. There's a bunch of personal stuff of his . . . a tennis racquet, towel, paperback book, and so forth. Nothing unusual. He still had his wallet in his pocket, so it was easy to rule out robbery as a motive.

And then it hit me.

Sometimes what is not there is at least as important as what is there. It takes training to remember that, and I'm embarrassed that in this case I didn't. But right here, right now, what was not in Danny Avery's car is not staring me directly in the face.

His cell phone.

I simply do not believe that Avery could have been on a stakeout, on a case that he had to at least suspect had some danger to it, and not have his cell phone with him. It could not have happened.

But the phone was not in the car, which means that the killer took it. He did not do so casually or without purpose; he didn't take Avery's wallet. The killer took the time, after firing a deadly shot, to risk detection by opening the door and finding the phone. There had to be a reason for that.

The original investigators should have picked up on this, but I've made similar mistakes in the past. They were focused on analyzing what evidence was in the car, and since the motive was clearly not robbery, they didn't think about what wasn't there.

I have no way of knowing or finding out what was on that phone, but I might be able to find out something else just as important, maybe more so.

I call Sam Willis. "Sam, I know you can get access to GPS locations in cell phones."

"No problem."

"Right. But how far back can you go? Can you tell me where a phone was at a particular time almost two years ago?"

"Absolutely; just takes a little more digging. Those things are never erased; they live in cyberland."

"Perfect." I tell him that I want to know where Danny Avery's phone went after he was killed.

"They took his phone?"

"Yes."

"Assholes." Then, "Do you know his phone number?"

"No."

"Okay, I'll get it. When do you need this information?"

"Yesterday."

"It's going to take a bit longer than that. But I'll do it as fast as I can."

IT'S BEEN TWO DAYS SINCE WE LEARNED THAT JACOB RICHARDSON WAS apparently taken on a one-way ride to the woods of northwest Jersey.

Based on media reports, or the lack of them, his being missing has not attracted police attention.

I'm not surprised his neighbors in Short Hills have not noticed his absence. The houses are far apart, and those kind of exclusive neighborhoods are often not close-knit, or at least that's how my biased eye sees it. He has also only lived there a couple of years, so maybe he hasn't made any close friendships in the area.

But one would think business associates, or family, would discover that he was mysteriously gone and would say something. Maybe they have and I just don't know it.

Or maybe they haven't.

So I call Pete and tell him that we have been interested in

Richardson and asking around about him. Probably because of our inquiries, we got an anonymous tip that he had been the victim of foul play.

As is true of pretty much everything I tell Pete, he thinks I'm bullshitting him, which I am. But he says he will check into it.

As soon as I get off the phone, Sam calls. "This you are not going to believe. Danny Avery's phone was taken out of town the night he was killed. Guess where it went."

"Philadelphia."

"Bingo . . . very impressive. You can move on to the next level. It went to a house in Bryn Mawr. You want to go double or nothing on your bet and guess who owns the house?"

"Arthur Rucker."

"Double bingo."

This is monster news. "Sam, what happened to the phone after that?"

"Absolutely nothing. It was at Rucker's house for less than thirty minutes and then went totally blank. Probably destroyed, but no way to know."

"Thanks, Sam. Great job. But of course I have something else for you. Is it possible to tell if other cell phones arrived at Rucker's house when Avery's did?"

Sam hesitates, which already is uncharacteristic. "Yes . . . it's possible."

"Is there a problem?"

"The data will be there, but it's old, so cross-checking the GPS signals could take quite a while. But I'll get on it."

"Thanks, Sam."

I immediately call Laurie to tell her this news about Avery's phone going to Rucker's house, and she is as blown away by it as I was.

"Game, set, and match," she says. "I need to get them to

issue a subpoena to get the GPS records. We can't hang Sam out to dry by using what he's gotten; we have to get it legally."

"Right; see if they can rush it."

We both agree that it's time to talk to Rucker, so I call Lieutenant Viola in Philadelphia. "I think it's time for you to repay the favor I did for you in removing Joey Wingate from the ranks of the living."

"Uh-oh. I don't like the sound of this."

"You might wind up thanking me again. I want to question Arthur Rucker. With you, in your interrogation room."

"I told you I'd need something new. I can't bring him in for the same old stuff; he'd have a decent harassment case against us."

"I know, and I have something very new. There's a possibility we can make Rucker for another murder . . . of a cop."

"You have my undivided attention."

"I told you about the cases we're working on. One of the three murder victims was a cop named Danny Avery. He was on a stakeout in a car when a shooter came up from behind and took him out.

"It was not a robbery; his wallet wasn't taken. But his phone was, and we've traced the GPS on that phone. It was taken to none other than Arthur Rucker's house in Philadelphia. Not soon after that it went off the grid."

"I would say that qualifies as something new. But why would Arthur Rucker have a New Jersey cop killed? Rucker is about money; how would your cop be a threat to his bottom line?"

"I wish I could tell you that. But Joey Wingate was here in the same area trying to, shall we say, deter me from further investigation, so obviously Rucker has a connection to all of this."

"I would say so. When shall we have our talk with Mr. Rucker?"

"Tomorrow would be good."

"I'll see what I can do, which means I'll make sure he's in town. If he is, we'll be chatting tomorrow. Though I can't say how talkative he'll be."

"Understood. Let me know if we're on."

My next call is to Pete. I haven't yet heard any feedback on Richardson being missing. It's not important to our case, since we already know what has happened to him, but I'm curious why it hasn't made any news.

"Nobody has seen him," Pete says. "But nobody has reported him missing either."

"That's strange. Are you searching for him?"

"I can't put out an APB for a rich guy who is gone for this short a time. He could be in Tahiti for all I know. I'm not aware of any evidence of foul play."

"Okay. But I have a feeling it's going to blow up."

"You've been wrong before."

"Not that I can recall."

I CONTINUE TO FIND IT CURIOUS THAT NO ONE HAS COME FORWARD TO say that Jacob Richardson seems to be missing.

I'm on the way to Philadelphia, so on the way I call Sam and ask, "When you were doing your research on Richardson, did you stumble on any members of his family? Any idea where they might be?"

"No, but that's not what I was looking for, so I wouldn't expect to have found any. You want me to look?"

"Yes, please do as thorough a job as you can of checking his background. I want to know where his family is, where old friends might be, what he had for breakfast every day for the last twenty years."

"Okay. I remember he was born here but grew up in Atlanta. I saw that on a business document he had to submit to a court last year."

"Good. That's the kind of stuff I need, but much more."

"And you need it in a hurry." It's a statement, not a question.

"I didn't say that."

"So you don't?"

"Of course I do."

The interrogation of Arthur Rucker is scheduled at Lieutenant Viola's precinct at 11:00 A.M. I get there at ten, in time for us to go over our approach.

The first issue is how I will be presented to Rucker and his attorney, who he has indicated will be coming with him. It's tricky because I am a civilian. Once we resolve that, we discuss the questioning, but only in short strokes, because Viola is basically going to be an observer.

When we enter the interrogation room, Rucker and his attorney, Gillian Naylor, are waiting. Rucker looks to be in his early fifties, balding on his head but not his upper lip. Right now, he's about four foot six, but that's because he is sitting down and makes no attempt to get up.

"Good morning," Viola says. "This is Detective Corey Douglas. He works for the Paterson, New Jersey, Police Department."

All of that is technically true, albeit meant to be deceptive.

"Paterson, New Jersey?" Rucker asks. "Where the hell is that?"

"I believe it is in New Jersey," Viola answers. I like her style. "Thank you for being here, Mr. Rucker. As in our previous sessions, this meeting is being recorded, video and audio. For the record, Mr. Rucker is accompanied by his attorney, Ms. Naylor. I am with Detective Douglas, who will be doing the questioning of Mr. Rucker."

"Understood," Ms. Naylor says. "Please also note for the record that Mr. Rucker is appearing voluntarily, for what is now the fourth time."

"So noted," Viola says. "Detective Douglas?"

My style in these settings is not to drone on, but rather to fire quick, short penetrating questions. Some subjects get intimidated by that, though I suspect Rucker will not be one of those people. And Naylor definitely won't be.

"Do you know Joseph Wingate? Nickname 'Icepick'?"

"Him again?" Rucker asks.

"Let's try and be responsive. It will move things along better. Do you know him?"

"Only by reputation and through this case. I know that he is a suspect in the murder of my former partner, Wilson Dozier."

"You've never met him?"

"No."

"Ever talked to him or communicated with him in any way?"

"No."

"Do you know why he would have killed Mr. Dozier?"

"I have no idea."

"You and Mr. Dozier had been in a business dispute, is that correct?"

Rucker is clearly frustrated. He turns to Viola. "I've answered these questions a million times."

"Then you should be good at it by now," I say. "Do you own an apartment at the Demarest Hotel in Chapin Falls, New York?"

He seems surprised by the abrupt change. "What? Yes, I do."

"How long have you owned it?"

"I don't remember exactly. Maybe three years?"

"Why did you decide to buy it?"

"I shouldn't have; it was a ridiculous purchase. You walk

in there, the lobby is filled with tourists and kids. You want to buy it?"

"Did you not understand the question?"

"Wilson . . . Dozier . . . he suggested it. He said he had been there and loved the place. He already had a place not that far from there, and he suggested I buy it. We could hold business meetings up there. That was before the bastard stabbed me in the back."

Rucker does not seem to hold his deceased former partner in high regard. "How often do you use the apartment?"

"Once a year, maybe. If that. I think I've spent three weeks there; I go when I find out the hotel is going to be fairly empty."

"Do you have the dates for the visits you've made?"

"I do; they would be on my calendars. But I don't have them with me."

"We can get you that information," says Naylor.

"Please do. Mr. Rucker, does the name Daniel Avery mean anything to you?"

"No. I don't think so."

"He was a police detective in Paterson, New Jersey. He was murdered in his car on February seventeenth, 2021."

"What is this? Now I'm supposed to have committed another murder? What am I, a serial killer? I'm not answering any more of these questions."

I nod. "That's perfectly within your rights. But since you're not familiar with Paterson, I should tell you that we convene grand juries there, and that you will be brought before one, under oath, to answer the same questions you're refusing to answer now. You'll love Paterson; it's a really friendly city."

"Give me a minute." He and Naylor whisper to each other. Then, "Okay, let's get this over with. I know nothing about this detective other than what you've told me."

"When he was killed, his phone was stolen. The data shows that three hours later the phone was brought to your house. Can you explain that—"

"That's bullshit."

"Where were you on April seventeenth, 2021?"

"How the hell should . . . did you say April seventeenth?"

"That's correct."

"I was in Las Vegas."

"You remember that without your calendar?"

"I go with friends to Vegas every year on April fifteenth. It's tax day; we used to say that we go to Vegas to lose whatever money we haven't given to the government. It's become a tradition for us; we go with our wives."

"You can provide proof of that? Credit card receipts, hotel bill?"

"Yeah, sure. Absolutely. And you can talk to my friends."

"When you are away on these trips, who would be staying at your house?"

"Nobody. The housekeeper goes there the day before we get home. But we would have come home later than the seventeenth."

I ask some additional questions, but do not get any more useful information. If he was intimidated or worried about the Demarest Hotel or Danny Avery, he hid it well. And it will be interesting to see what proof he can come up with.

The key point is that I know he is lying. Avery's phone didn't accidentally go to the wrong house that night; and whether Rucker was home or not, it is still highly incriminating. Rucker could have had some of his people there to receive it.

Also, Jimmy Dietrich did not coincidentally go to the hotel in upstate New York where Rucker happened to have an apartment. Rucker's prints are all over this case.

But proving he is lying may continue to be rather difficult. Rucker is sophisticated and seems to have effectively covered his tracks.

He is still well more than one step ahead of us.

AMONG THE MANY THINGS I WISH I KNEW, NEAR THE TOP OF THE LIST IS why Arthur Rucker wanted Danny Avery's phone.

The police already had Danny's emails and text messages from back around that time; they were on his computer and iPad. Rucker would have known that merely taking the phone would not have prevented the authorities from accessing those things. Not only that, but there obviously was not anything on there that was incriminating to him.

But clearly something had to be on that phone that made it worth it to the killer to stop and retrieve it after firing the fatal shot.

Rucker is a practiced liar. I'm sure he will produce documents and records supporting his alibi, and I'm also sure that they will be bullshit. But my guess is that cutting through it is going to be difficult.

Laurie asks Pete to assign his cyber experts to see about getting anything of Danny's phone that might be in the cloud. Since I don't have the slightest clue what the hell the cloud is, I have no point of view on it either way.

Sam tells Laurie and me that it's a waste of time; that even if there is anything there, Apple won't provide it, because of their privacy concerns. Fighting it out in the courts is simply not going to lead anywhere; it's been adjudicated before and nothing happens.

"But the strange thing is that whoever took the phone and brought it to Rucker . . . they wouldn't have been able to get anything off of it either," Sam says. "It would have been protected, either by face ID or fingerprint, and a code. Unless Avery told them the code before he got shot, the phone would have been useless to them."

"I don't think so, Sam," I say. "It's possible that they weren't looking to get anything off the phone; the point could have been to keep it away from the authorities."

Sam shakes his head. "The cops couldn't have opened it either."

"Maybe Susan Avery knew her husband's code," Laurie says. "In any event, they might not have thought that far ahead or wanted to take any chances. If they had the phone, then the cops didn't."

"But if that was their goal, then why bring the phone to Rucker, or whoever was at his house? And then destroy it? Why not just destroy it at the scene?" I ask.

"I suppose they didn't think about the problems they'd have getting anything off it," Laurie says. "Or maybe they were hoping Avery had no protection on the phone, and they could just open it."

I place a call to Steven Barkley, the owner/manager of the

Demarest Hotel. It seems like I'm always on the phone or in the car, often at the same time.

He starts off the call with an apology. "I'm sorry, Detective, I'm drawing a blank on anything suspicious that I've come across. And I've confidentially asked a couple of my top executives, who had nothing to offer either."

"I wasn't calling for a report. I have a few more questions."

"Anything I can do."

"Are you familiar with Arthur Rucker?"

"Arthur? Of course. He's one of the owners of the apartments on the eighth floor. Doesn't use it very often, though."

"When was he there last?"

"I don't know the answer to that."

"Can I get a list of the dates he has been there in the last two years?"

"Detective, first of all, he owns the apartment, so he doesn't have to check in to the hotel. So he could certainly be there without me being aware of it. But also, I don't feel comfortable reporting on the movements of our residents."

"We can subpoena that information."

"Then I think it's best you do that. I'm not trying to be difficult, but I'm concerned about the ethics here, to say nothing of the legalities. I can check with our counsel as well, which I will do."

"Can you tell me if he usually comes there alone?"

"Yes, I believe so. Though as I recall he often has people visit him here; he leaves instructions with the security guard at the elevator."

I thank Barkley and get off the phone. I find Rucker's having visitors at the hotel to be interesting. The Demarest is not exactly in Midtown Manhattan, and Rucker is from Philadelphia. Who would he entertain there?

I head home, and Dani and Simon are there to greet me. I don't see Marcus anywhere, but I know he's been watching out for Dani when I'm not home. Invisibility is another of Marcus's superhero talents.

Tonight, Dani, Simon, and I are going to dinner, which will be nice. I'm planning to pretend that a lovely night out will help take my mind off the case.

Of course, it doesn't. Dani asks how things are going, which sets me off. I bring her up to date, and the difference between us immediately comes into focus.

She thinks we've made amazing progress, particularly by identifying Rucker as our key suspect. I, being Mr. Negative, can only focus on that which we don't know and can't prove.

I lay it out for Dani in the hope that maybe just by talking about it clarity will come crashing through. I start with the negatives, with what we haven't figured out.

"We still don't know why Danny Avery was watching Jacob Richardson and George Hafner at that restaurant, or what Avery was onto. We don't know why Jimmy Dietrich flew to Chicago to interview Kathy Linder, whose husband embezzled all that money and took off. We don't know why Jimmy was interested in Ian Solis, the computer guy that the FBI and Homeland Security are after. Should I go on?"

"Please do."

"We don't know why the killer wanted Danny Avery's phone. We don't know why they have apparently killed Jacob Richardson. We don't know why Rucker has to go to the Demarest Hotel in the middle of nowhere to have meetings.

"And to top it all off, we don't know what Rucker, and any accomplices he might have, are doing. Why the conspiracy? He had his partner, Wilson Dozier, killed. I get that. But why wasn't that it? Why all these other pieces?"

"Wow" is all Dani can say.

"Now you want the list of things we do know? It's much shorter."

"Sure."

"We know Arthur Rucker is at the center of all of this, and we know all the pieces are somehow connected. That's it." I'm exaggerating our bewilderment, but not by much.

"You want my view on this? As an uninformed civilian?"

"I do."

"All these pieces, it's like when you set up a string of dominoes in a row. You tip the first one over, and it knocks all the others down, one by one."

"That's a little obscure for me."

"You need to answer the first question; What was Danny Avery doing on that street, and what was he trying to accomplish? Once you get that, the other dominoes will fall."

"That's what Laurie said."

"Of course. Did you ever notice how much smarter women are than men? With the exception of Simon, of course."

Simon is having dinner under the table, a plate of mixed grilled vegetables, so he doesn't react to his name being mentioned. He has his priorities.

"I have noticed that. And you're right; it has always started with Avery's involvement. But we've been trying to figure that out since day one, and we've gotten nowhere. You have any suggestions?"

"Hey, it's my job to pose the questions, and your job to answer them. Let's stay in our own lanes."

SO IT'S BACK TO THE DRAWING BOARD, OR IN THIS CASE THE POLICE reports.

My first reread of the Danny Avery files triggered my noticing that his phone was stolen, which eventually led to Arthur Rucker. So since that is my version of being on a roll, I'm going back to the same files in the hope of generating a new inspiration.

Unfortunately, it doesn't work out. The rest of the murder file tells me nothing I don't already know. Undaunted, I pick up the file on the domestic violence incident in which Avery killed Frank Gilmore. I haven't read this one in a long time, mainly because it's only tangentially related to our case.

Vince Petri, who we believe killed Avery, was allegedly a friend of Gilmore's. He was one of the "hoodlum" friends that Julie Simonson described, while at the same time she and everybody else say that the wealthy Gilmore had another side to him, a far more respectable side.

The case seemed to signify a turning point in Avery's police career. That Gilmore had no prior arrests or difficulties with the law, coupled with his reputation as a successful businessman, led some people to think that perhaps Avery had been trigger-happy.

Other people looked at the bruises Gilmore inflicted on Julie Simonson and sided with Avery, but the controversy damaged Avery's standing in the department. He was cleared by an independent review board, but the stain remained, and by all accounts he was embittered by it. I would have been angry also if it had happened to me.

I'm interested in Gilmore only because the domestic violence shooting was such a significant event in Avery's life that perhaps it somehow impacted what he was doing afterward.

I reread the reports on the domestic violence event but learn nothing new. Avery and Gilmore were alone in the room when it happened; Avery's partner had taken an upset and injured Julie Simonson into another room to shield her. It is as she described it to me.

Because of the way it went down, only Avery and Gilmore knew what happened, and neither are around to present their case any further. But Gilmore had been brandishing a gun, and Avery was thus able to make an effective case to the review board that he had acted in self-defense.

I've been interested throughout in the Jekyll and Hyde aspect to Gilmore. Julie spoke about this from a personality standpoint, but it also manifested itself in the friends he had. He hung around with Vince Petri and people from that world, but on the flip side he was a businessman who kept company with an entirely different class of people.

I start reading about Gilmore's business life and am immediately jolted. Gilmore is listed as being involved with three businesses, but it's the first one that knocks me on my ass. He was the chief executive of a company called FGI.

I check my notes to confirm, and there it is. Sam Willis had described Jacob Richardson's company, which funded start-ups, as a borderline shell company that had only provided limited funding to three start-ups.

One of those was FGI, the *FG* now obviously standing for Frank Gilmore. I hadn't noticed it before because the last time I read through this file was well before Sam told me the list of Richardson's investments.

This represents, in my eyes, a stunning development. It connects Gilmore to Richardson, which at least begins to explain why Danny Avery was on that street watching for Richardson and George Hafner to come out of the restaurant.

I call Laurie to discuss what I've found.

She completely agrees that this is a major breakthrough: "Danny Avery was trying to further justify his actions the night he shot Gilmore. He was proving that Gilmore was not some innocent businessman caught in a bad moment, but that he was a bad guy all along."

"Right. He was investigating Gilmore and found out something important, something that tied him into a major conspiracy."

"I wonder who else Gilmore was tied into. It seems like all the pieces were connected, leading up to Arthur Rucker. The more we can figure out how these players were related to each other, the easier it will be to figure out what the hell was going on."

"I'm going to call Julie Simonson," I say.

"You think she'll know something?"

"No downside to finding out."

"True. In the meantime, I'll try and find other friends of Gilmore to see if they can tell us anything."

I call Julie at the supermarket that she manages. She doesn't sound thrilled to hear from me, but she's polite about it. She wants to put anything related to Frank Gilmore and that time of her life behind her, but I keep preventing that from happening.

"I just need to bother you one more time," I say, probably lying. The truth is that I will bother her as many times as necessary, and each time I'll promise that it will be the last time.

"I've really told you everything I know."

"I just want to show you some photographs, so you can tell me if you recognize any of the people in them."

She hesitates, so I add, "There's a kale salad in it for you."

She laughs and says that she'll meet me at the diner in an hour. I'm a real charmer.

I gather up the photographs that I have, from all the files, of everyone that the investigation has touched on. I include everyone because, even if someone has no obvious connection to Gilmore, we keep discovering interconnections between people that surprise us.

We sit down and order; I again go with the hamburger, which was fine last time and which is the closest to the opposite of kale that I can think of. We make some small talk; mostly about her job. She tells me that supply-chain issues are making it difficult to keep the store well stocked.

Then it's my turn to talk about my job, so I open the envelope I brought with me. "You said last time that you are terrible on names but great remembering faces."

She smiles. "I don't think I said 'great,' but I'm pretty good at it."

I show her the photos one at a time. The first one is of George Hafner.

She stares at it intently. "No."

I show her Jacob Richardson. "No," she says, disappointing me.

Then Roger Linder, the Chicago embezzler. "No."

Then Arthur Rucker. "No." This is not going well.

Next is potential cyberterrorist Ian Solis. "No."

Next is Vince Petri. "No."

Joey Wingate. "No."

Then Wilson Dozier, Rucker's partner, who was killed by Wingate, probably at Rucker's direction. "Yes, I recognize him."

Whoa. "Are you sure?"

"Yes, I'm positive. He was at Frank's apartment. He was leaving when I arrived. I said hello, but he just walked by me. It was rude, and Frank explained by saying they were having a business problem."

"Do you know anything else about him? Did Frank say anything?"

"Not that I remember."

"When would this have been?"

She takes some time and figures it out. She tells me a date as close as she can estimate, and it's about a month before Dozier became, to use Joy Viola's phrase, "shark food."

I'm anxious to get out of here and discuss this with Laurie, but I don't feel comfortable saying, "Hurry up and finish that damn kale." But I don't have any more photographs to show her, and don't want to ask any more questions.

I don't want her talking. I want her chewing.

SO FRANK GILMORE NOT ONLY HAD A CONNECTION TO JACOB RICHARD-son, he also had one to Wilson Dozier.

Dozier, a Philadelphia businessman, was in Gilmore's apartment not long before he was murdered. Julie Simonson said she was sure of it.

"So here's my theory," Laurie says. "Rucker and Dozier were not just partners in that computer chip company. They were also partners in whatever this illegal conspiracy was. But they had a falling out, and Rucker had him killed. And Gilmore and Richardson were also involved, in some way that is unclear at the moment."

"Makes as much sense as anything else I can come up with," I say. "And we can lump George Hafner in there as well. His murder was not a coincidence."

"The only people we haven't linked to Gilmore are Ian Solis and Roger Linder. But I'll bet we do that before this is over."

"I hope so. And Gilmore was the entry point for Danny Avery. He was investigating Gilmore, probably hoping to show that he was not the above-reproach philanthropist that some people saw him as. Whatever he found led him into this world and got him killed."

"And the same thing killed Jimmy and Susan Avery as well, because they started out by retracing Danny's steps," Laurie says.

"One thing that all the players seem to have in common is that they had money . . . a lot of it. So whatever they were doing together had to involve major bucks. They certainly weren't above killing for it."

"I know Gilmore and Richardson were from this area, but whatever is going on is national. Marcus has been working the streets and not coming up with anything. Rucker and Dozier were from Philly, Linder from Chicago, Solis from California. . . . I think Danny Avery was uncovering something much wider than maybe even he knew."

"And Rucker is sitting in Philadelphia laughing at us," I say. "We need to find a way to draw him out."

My phone rings and I can see from the caller ID that it's Lieutenant Viola in Philadelphia. "Maybe I can get her to kill Rucker," I say before picking up. "She must know some hit men in Philly."

But I don't open with that joking request; instead I just say, "Hello," and wait to hear what she wants.

"Rucker has supplied receipts from Vegas, and a list of his friends who will swear he was there with them on the day your friend was killed."

"Doesn't surprise me." It doesn't. "Could be one of two things. Either the receipts and alibi are somehow bullshit, or someone else was at his house that night. But he wasn't running a bed-and-breakfast; whoever was there was working for him."

"You New Jersey guys aren't very trusting."

"I've been told that before. How do you read it?"

"Pretty much the same. I don't know that much about your case, though the phone showing up at his house is obviously incriminating. But I believe Rucker killed Dozier, so I'm not inclined to give him the benefit of the doubt."

"Any chance you can just shoot him? Then we can move on to the next case."

She laughs. "Let me see what I can do."

I get off the call and turn to Laurie. "I don't think she's going to shoot him. You think Marcus would do the job?"

"No, I think this one is on you."

The phone rings, and Laurie gets it. After "Hi, Sam," she pauses for a short while, then says, "Why?"

His response must have been satisfactory because she says, "Okay, we're on our way."

She gets off. "Come on, Sam wants us to meet him at Barnert Hospital."

"Is he okay?"

"Sounds like it. He wasn't too clear, but said he needs us down there."

"He's not hurt?"

"Corey, I have told you everything I know."

"You think I can bring Simon?"

"To a hospital?"

"Why not? I'll bet he's cleaner than half the doctors there."

"Leave him here. Andy and Tara can entertain him."

SAM IS WAITING FOR US AT THE ENTRANCE TO BARNERT HOSPITAL WHEN we pull up.

Actually, Barnert Hospital is not really a hospital, not anymore. It used to be, but then ran into financial trouble and went bankrupt. It reopened later as what is called a Medical Arts Complex, which I guess means it's an okay place to go if you're feeling sick, but not if you are looking to have open-heart surgery.

We park and get out. Sam looks to be in good health, so fortunately that concern is out the window. "What's going on, Sam?"

"It's about Richardson. I was doing a deep dive into his life, and I found a copy of his birth certificate, which showed he was born at Barnert. Remember I told you he was born here but grew up in Atlanta?"

"Yes," Laurie says.

"Well, the birth certificate looked normal, but then I

noticed that there was no official seal on it. That seemed strange, so I came down here to ask them to check their records. It seemed easier than getting into their system, just for that one thing."

"What did they say?"

"Come on, hear it for yourself. She won't tell me. She's nervous about something and will only talk to the detectives. That's you."

We follow him in. Some people are sitting along the wall, apparently waiting to be called in to a doctor. Two women are behind the reception desk. One of them, probably in her late sixties, is dealing with one person. The other person has no one to wait on.

But we wait for the occupied person to finish; clearly she is the one that Sam wants us to talk to.

After a few long minutes, she's free and we approach the desk. "These are the people I told you about, Ms. Larson. Detectives Collins and Douglas."

"I'm not sure I should be doing this," she says.

"You're not doing anything wrong," Sam says. "And it's urgent."

She nods. "Okay . . . I guess so." She turns to Sam. "The copy of the birth certificate you showed me is not a real one."

Sam takes it out and puts it on the desk.

"So it's not in your system?" Laurie asks.

"No, it's in the system. I found it right away."

"Then how do you know it's not real? Because there is no seal?" I ask.

"Yes, probably, but that happens. Things can get pretty hectic, and people make mistakes."

Sam prompts her, "You said there was something else that you would share when they got here."

She hesitates; she can probably see herself testifying in court and doesn't like the idea. "Well, when I looked it up, I noticed something strange. There was a three-week period . . ." She points to the date on the birth certificate. "Two weeks before this date and a week after . . . this was the only birth certificate in the system for that whole period."

"Is that not possible?" I ask.

"This was a very busy hospital back then, and the maternity ward was very active. It was a different world. There is no chance there could have been only one birth in three weeks."

"So how do you explain it?" Laurie asks.

"I couldn't figure it out myself, so I looked into it. And I was actually working here back then; that gives you an idea how old I am."

"Child labor," I say, ever the charmer.

She smiles. "Afraid not. Anyway, we had a fire back then; it started in the cafeteria. There wasn't a lot of physical damage, but the smoke caused a lot of problems. The hospital was closed for three weeks; all the patients were transferred to St. Joseph's and Paterson General. Those are the same three weeks we are talking about."

"Ah." Sam nods.

"So it's not possible that Jacob Richardson was born here on the date of this birth certificate?" Laurie asks.

"Unless the mother snuck in and gave birth in the dark without a doctor, it's not possible."

WE HEAD BACK TO LAURIE'S HOUSE TO TRY TO FIGURE OUT WHAT THIS means.

Andy is there when we arrive, so we invite him to join in the discussion. The more minds looking at this the better.

"So let's assume that there's no mistake made here, that the birth certificate is inaccurate, and Richardson was not born in that hospital on that day," Laurie says.

"There's no mistake," I say. "In addition to the fire, there is no seal on the certificate. It's not real; I don't think there's any doubt about that.

"And no one has reported him missing in all this time, ever since he was taken up to the woods. I found that strange, but this explains it. No one knows where he is; no one even knows who he is. That's how he wanted it."

"Okay, so he's operating under an alias," Laurie says. "Why do people do that?"

Andy answers, "A lot of reasons. But the most common is that he's wanted somewhere for something."

Laurie nods. "So we need a DNA sample, which will be tough because he's gone and not coming back."

"No problem," I say. "I'll get one. I'll go back to his house tonight; it will be filled with his DNA. Hairbrush, toothbrush, it will be a DNA festival. I'll have no trouble getting a sample."

"You're going to break in?"

"Not necessary. When Sam and I were there, the door was open. I doubt anybody has been there since to lock it."

"Okay, great," Laurie says. "I'll call Alvarez in Forensics and tell him we need a rush put on it. He owes me about ten favors. Of course, I owe him about twenty, but he'll overlook that."

"I think we've got a plan," I say.

I head home for dinner with Dani and Simon. Since I don't have a lot of time tonight, and since neither Dani nor I want to risk one of us cooking dinner, I stop on the way home to pick up pizza and salads.

While we're eating, I tell her my plans for the evening. "You want to go with me?"

"Do I want to go with you to break into a house to steal a toothbrush?"

"The way you say it, it doesn't sound that glamorous. But that's pretty much it, yeah."

"Life with you gets more exciting every day, but, no, I think I'll go over to Denise's for coffee. That way Marcus doesn't have to watch me."

"You know about that?" I hadn't told her about Marcus; I was afraid she might resist it.

"Of course. You're not exactly tough to figure out, you know? But listen, when you go to get the toothbrush, I could use a new hairbrush. Why don't you steal one of those while you're there?"

"I can do that." Then, "Simon, you want to come for a ride?"

Simon doesn't say no, so I'll take it as a yes.

So Simon and I drive Dani to her friend Denise's house, then head out to Jacob Richardson's house in Short Hills. Actually, I don't know whose house it is now. We know that Richardson won't have any more use for it, and since we can't locate any family, I wonder who he's left it to.

If he hasn't done a will, maybe Simon, Dani, and I should just move in and claim squatter's rights. It's a nice house; we could be comfortable there.

We pull into the long driveway. It's dark here; no lights are on inside or outside the house because there is no living owner to turn them on. We park behind the house; no reason that we should attract the attention of a neighbor who might see the car.

We walk around to the front and go in through the front door, just as I did when I was here with Sam. It's hard to see, so I turn on one lamp. We make our way upstairs to what seems to be the master bedroom and go into the bathroom off that.

This place is DNA central. I grab a toothbrush and a hairbrush with a lot of hairs stuck in it. Then I take the small drinking glass on the sink; he probably used it to rinse the toothpaste out of his mouth. I put everything into small plastic zipper bags that I brought for the occasion.

When I go back down, I take a few minutes to look around. Everything is exactly as I saw it when I was here with Sam; I would bet that no one has been here in the interim.

I turn the lamp off and we exit through the front door; this has to be the weirdest burglary I have ever been associated with. We head back down the dark driveway and are halfway to our car when Simon stops cold.

Something has alerted him.

"Not another step, dipshit."

I see a shadow come out from the side of the house. If I'm not mistaken, and I hope I am, I see a slight glint of light off what seems to be a gun in his hand.

I have learned that in a situation like this, the first move is everything. It must be aggressive and timed to the initial jolt of adrenaline. Once the situation settles in, the assailant has all the advantage, so I need to change that dynamic immediately.

"Get!"

Simon has a number of advantages as a partner, and just as many as a weapon. One is that he's silent; he's been trained that way. No growling, no barking, when he's attacking.

For another, he's ruthless. He wasn't born with a "mercy" gene; this dog when working does not have a conscience.

In the dark, I doubt that this guy sees Simon, and when he finally senses that an airborne canine missile is coming toward him, it's too late. Simon has better aim than an accomplished sniper, and while still in midair, he chomps onto the wrist on the gun hand.

The guy screams in pain as I move toward him. I'm almost on him when I hear the gun hit the pavement. The first thing I do is punch him in the face; based on the sound and how much it hurts my hand, I think I've broken his cheekbone.

I have a gun but I do not want to shoot him; I want him alive so he can be questioned. I briefly reconsider that decision when he punches me back, landing a glancing blow to my face. Of course, he's at a disadvantage; it's hard to fight when one of your arms is being chewed on by a German shepherd. At the very least, it's distracting.

"Simon, off!" I yell, and Simon obeys. I don't want any help; I don't need any.

So we fight, and the guy lands a few good shots. I land more than a few, and I have the upper hand. Then, behind him, I see something that shocks me.

Marcus.

He's not doing anything; just standing and watching. I don't know what to make of that, and I look forward to finding out.

I end the fight by punching the guy in the neck. He goes down, gasping and making choking noises. When we finally ask him questions, I think he's going to have to answer in writing.

I grab my phone and call Pete Stanton. I don't want Short Hills cops to come to the scene; they might have trouble identifying who the good guys are. While I'm talking, I see that Marcus has turned the guy facedown and is handcuffing his arms behind him. I didn't realize Marcus carried handcuffs.

I get off the call and turn to Marcus. "What are you doing here?"

"Laurie said you were coming here and told me to watch out for you."

"Did she tell you to intervene? Or just watch?"

"I would have stopped him if you couldn't. But you could, and it was entertaining."

"I'm glad you enjoyed yourself."

PETE HANDLED IT LAST NIGHT JUST LIKE I HOPED HE WOULD.

He came to the scene with four cops, took the guy into custody, got some basic information, and told me to come see him in the morning. The entire thing took less than twenty minutes. If the Short Hills cops had come and didn't shoot us by mistake, I wouldn't have gotten out of there until three in the morning.

When Simon and I got home, I debated whether to tell Dani what happened. At some point she might decide that a long-term future is unlikely with someone who people are constantly trying to kill. Certainly she would never want to M such a person, and who could blame her?

But I told her anyway. I decided to be honest, not because I have any particular respect for personal honesty. I mean, I think it's generally the way to go, but certain factors could call for a different approach. In this case, I thought she deserved the truth.

My honesty also came from an inability to explain away the bruises on my face. All I was doing was going to pick up a toothbrush; people do things like that all the time without getting in fights.

She made me describe exactly what happened. I would have exaggerated the heroism in my performance, but Simon was right there and might have felt slighted. "But at least I did more than Marcus," I say in finishing the story.

"Why didn't he get involved?"

"He was apparently enjoying the show."

So now I'm in Pete's office, preparing to answer his questions about what the hell is going on. I also owe him as much honesty as I can come up with because he violated a bunch of protocols last night to help me.

For one thing, the incident was out of his jurisdiction; he's not a Short Hills cop. But he knows a captain in that department and said that he's sure he can smooth it over. Even so, the decision held some risk.

Furthermore, Pete is the captain of the Homicide Division, and the incident last night was not a homicide. I suspect that if the guy we took into custody had had his way, it would have been. But technically, Pete should have referred it to the proper division, which would in turn have let the Short Hills PD handle it.

"Let's start with, What the hell were you doing there?" Pete asks.

"I was getting a DNA sample of Richardson's."

"Was he home?"

"Of course not."

"So let me understand this . . . you broke into his house?"

"Technically, I suppose that's true. But the door was open, and I confirmed a bunch of times that he was not home. He will never be home again, Pete. The guy is dead."

"You know that?"

I nod. "Trust me."

"So why did you need a DNA sample? Have you found a body? Because I'm not aware of any report to that effect. Do you have him cut up in your freezer?"

"No, Pete . . . I doubt anyone will ever find the body. My goal was to find out who Jacob Richardson is. Because he's not Jacob Richardson. That much is certain."

I go on to explain why I believe that, including the birth certificate story. He doesn't seem completely convinced, but asks, "Where's the sample now?"

"Laurie dropped it off with Forensics. We'll have an answer in a couple of days."

"It takes me a week to get a DNA report back. And that's on a rush basis."

"Laurie's nicer than you. And better looking. Much better looking."

"Maybe you can get her to run the DNA of the asshole you beat up last night."

"You don't know who he is?"

"No. No ID on him, and he won't say a word. Not asking for a lawyer, but not talking. Actually, I doubt he can talk; you messed up his neck pretty good. But all in all he seems like a fun guy. We're running his prints now."

"He has a good right cross. Left jab is a little weak."

"So write out your statement when we're done here. Leave out the part about Laurie being better looking than me. How are things on the cases you're allegedly trying to solve for us?"

"We're getting there. We're confident that Vince Petri killed Danny Avery, but we're not sure who gave the order. It definitely was not Petri avenging his friend Frank Gilmore's death because of their deep relationship."

"What about Jimmy Dietrich and Susan Avery?"

"There the opposite is true. We don't know who killed them, but we know who ordered it."

"Who might that be?"

"Arthur Rucker. He's from Philly, and—"

Pete interrupts, "Did you say Arthur Rucker?"

"I did. Do you know him?"

"We got back the information we subpoenaed from the phone company about where Danny Avery's phone went the night he was killed."

I nod. "Arthur Rucker's house."

"You knew that?"

"Wild guess. Based on that, can we take him into custody here? I have a cop in Philly who would be more than happy to cooperate."

Pete thinks about it for a few moments. "Do we know if he has an alibi for that night?"

"It happens that he does, but it has not been scrutinized carefully yet."

"That makes it more difficult. I would be shocked if we could get the prosecutor to authorize an arrest based on the movement of a phone, and I'm not sure we should try at this point. Let's wait until we have more."

"Getting more is proving difficult."

"That's why we pay you the big bucks," Pete says, a big smile on his face.

TO SAY WE'VE MADE NO PROGRESS IN THE LAST TWO DAYS WOULD BE giving us too much credit.

We're just running in place, going over what we have learned and trying to fit it into some coherent theory of a conspiracy. We believe strongly, along with the Philadelphia cops, that Arthur Rucker is a murderer, that he had his partner, Wilson Dozier, killed.

I'd also bet good money that he is responsible for at least the deaths of Jimmy Dietrich, Susan Avery, George Hafner, and whoever Jacob Richardson really is. And the two attempts on my life have Rucker's fingerprints all over them as well.

But today is hopefully a new day, and I've just gotten to Laurie's house. Actually, I've beaten her here by about a half hour, which gave me time to lose a video game to Ricky, Andy and Laurie's son. Andy looked on happily as I got crushed and shared with me that he's lost fourteen games in a row to Ricky.

"But I put up a better fight than you," Andy says.

Laurie mercifully comes back before we can start a second game. She's been down at Paterson PD, getting the DNA results for Jacob Richardson and the fingerprint results on the guy who attacked me at Richardson's house.

"Let's start with the bad news," she says. "Richardson's DNA did not generate a hit."

Both Andy and I are surprised by this. It's definitely bad news; it means that whoever Richardson is, he was never charged with a crime, nor did he serve in the military. That will make it infinitely harder to identify him.

"I was sure he was on the run," Andy says.

Andy's comment rings some kind of bell in the deep recesses of my mind, but I can't connect to what it is, or if it's anything at all.

'Well, he wasn't," Laurie says. "So we're nowhere."

"I could get fingerprints from the house, but that wouldn't help. If he wasn't in the DNA registry, his fingerprints wouldn't be on file either."

Laurie and Andy nod their agreement, so I say, "You said you were starting with the bad news. What's the good news?"

"I didn't say there was good news, but the rest isn't as bad as Richardson. The guy at the house the other night, who by the way still isn't saying a word, goes by the name Sonny Davenport."

"Who is he?"

"He's hired muscle out of Philadelphia."

"The long arm of Arthur Rucker strikes again," I say. "That guy is getting on my nerves."

"There's a warrant out for Davenport for assault with a deadly weapon. It's six months old."

I call Lieutenant Viola in Philadelphia. After brief small talk, I say, "There was another attempt made on my life."

"I'm sorry to hear that. Clearly it failed, or we wouldn't be having this conversation, but were you hurt?"

"No, I prevailed. The piece of garbage that I prevailed against is named Sonny Davenport."

"I know Sonny Davenport; he's wanted here. 'Piece of garbage' doesn't fully capture his charm."

"Did I offend your city in some way? People from there keep trying to kill me."

"Maybe it's your personality, or are you a Mets fan?"

"Or maybe it's Rucker."

"I wouldn't be surprised. Did Davenport survive your encounter?"

"He did. He's injured, but not talking. We'd like to keep him here for a while, in case he changes his mind."

"Unlikely."

"I know. But can you hold off on extraditing him for the time being?"

"For you? Anything. I'll make the necessary arrangements. Just tell me when you're done with him, and we'll welcome him home."

"Thanks. There's one other thing. We've connected Wilson Dozier to one of the probable bad guys in our investigation, Frank Gilmore. He was seen with him almost a month before Dozier died."

"Another interesting development. You're full of them."

"Definitely. Is it possible that Dozier and Rucker were partners beyond the chip company? Could they also have been in some kind of a criminal conspiracy together?"

"No reason why not. And then when they had their falling out, it was another reason for Rucker to kill him."

"Right. I can't think of another reason for Dozier to have been with Gilmore other than that he was part of the conspiracy."

"Conspiracy to do what?"

"Why must you ask questions like that? We were having such a pleasant conversation."

Viola laughs. "Let me know when you know."

I get off the phone and say to Laurie, "We have to find out who Richardson really was."

"I agree. But I don't know how we do that. And just knowing that won't get us to where we want to go."

"What do you mean?"

"Whatever we're dealing with, Richardson was not at the top of it. He was a piece, but the fact that they killed him means he was an expendable piece."

Then it hits me. "I may know who he was."

THE TIME WAS COMING; IAN SOLIS HAD LONG THOUGHT OF THIS MOMENT as the beginning of the end.

He would pick up the phone and make a simple call, and after that call nothing else would be the same.

They would have to give him the fortune he was demanding; that much was certain. He would be transparent. He would tell them how to search for his handiwork and show them how they were helpless to stop it.

When they had caved to his demands, he would decide what to do. He could renege on his agreement and take down the grid or honor it and leave it alone. Reneging held the most appeal for him, but that could change.

Either way he would become the most wanted man ever, certainly in this country and maybe the world. But that did not worry him in the slightest.

It had not been easy to get to this point. It took tireless

effort, probing and retreating, searching for the weaknesses he knew had to be there. Finally he had found them.

These two and half years had not been unrewarding. He and his partners had made a small fortune and developed a foolproof . . . well . . . it was almost like a new industry. Certainly a new area of expertise, which became a lucrative business.

But his partners had no idea what he had been doing all this time. They would soon be as surprised as everybody else.

Yet, while completely unaware, everything they had done together had led to this moment.

This is what it was all about.

Solis picked up the phone and dialed the number for Homeland Security in Washington, D.C. He had routed the call through a dizzying array of numbers and locations; it would appear to the government techs that this call originated in Iran.

When the operator answered, he simply said, "This is Ian Solis. Let me speak to the asshole in charge."

I DON'T THINK I'VE EVER HAD AN IDEA, NO MATTER HOW GOOD, WITHOUT being annoyed that I didn't come up with it earlier.

This is a perfect example of it. I should have realized much sooner the very real possibility that Jacob Richardson was really Roger Linder.

It all fits. Linder disappeared from his Chicago life around the same time that Richardson appeared in New Jersey. Linder got away with a fortune in embezzled money, which explains Richardson's wealth despite the fact that his New Jersey business appears to have been a shell company.

That Richardson's DNA did not generate a match also fits this scenario; Linder was never even accused of a crime until he had long left Chicago, and because he was never arrested and charged, his DNA would never have been put into the system.

Lastly, it explains the connection he had with George Hafner, and why they were having dinner together. Hafner was said to be a genius at creating fraudulent documents, the kind of documents that Richardson would have needed to maintain his fake identity.

I'm feeling excited and confident that I'm right about this, and I have a way to confirm it.

I call Kathy Linder in Chicago, and she is quick to say, "Do you have any information about Roger?"

"It's possible. I'm not sure, which is why I'm calling. I need your help." I'm not looking forward to breaking the news to her that Roger is dead; while she seems to believe she is long over him, that's not the feeling I'm getting. Since we have never confirmed Richardson's death, I probably shouldn't go there at all.

"How can I help?"

"I want to email you a photograph. It might be Roger, but it might not. I need you to tell me one way or the other if it's him."

"Where is this person?"

"Whoever it is has a house in New Jersey, but let's wait to see if it's Roger before I tell you any more."

"Okay. When are you sending it?"

"In just a couple of minutes. Give me your email address."

She does, and I tell her the phone number here. She promises to wait by her computer and call as soon as she receives it.

Laurie, meanwhile, has been scanning the photograph we have of Richardson into her computer, so we can send the email. If not for Laurie, I'd have to find Dani to do it. Since Dani is back in Vegas for a couple of days, I'd have to drive the damn picture to Chicago because there is no way I would know how to scan it.

When I drove Dani to the airport, I told her to be careful. Left unsaid was that the bad guys we are dealing with have a long reach. She smiled and said that she was so careful she made the reservation under a different name, so as to avoid any unwanted attention.

"What name did you use?"

"Kim Kardashian."

Once Laurie is finished with the scan and putting it into an email, I use my expertise to hit Send. Then we wait.

It doesn't take long. Maybe thirty seconds after I sent the email, the phone rings, and I can tell by the caller ID that it's Kathy Linder. She doesn't bother with saying "Hello."

All she says is "That's not Roger. Maybe a slight resemblance, but it's definitely not him."

She sounds terribly disappointed, a reaction that I share. I was positive I was right about this one. It wouldn't have solved our problems; we still wouldn't have known what Richardson's role in the conspiracy was. And we certainly wouldn't have understood the conspiracy itself.

But it would have been a step forward, and we haven't had many of those lately. On one level, a personal one for me, our work has had success. It has convinced me, beyond a shadow of a doubt, that Jimmy Dietrich did not kill Susan Avery, and he did not kill himself.

I wish I could feel relief about that, and maybe someday I will, but it seems a long way off. All I can think about is Arthur Rucker, and that he has so far gotten away with murder, and probably a lot more.

Simon and I head home. While I'm in the car, Sam calls. "I finally got that phone information."

"Which phone information is that?"

"You asked me to find out if any other cell phones accompanied Avery's to Rucker's house that night."

I had forgotten that I even made the request, but fortunately Sam doesn't forget anything. "What did you find out?"

"Well, there's absolutely another phone involved. It wasn't at the murder scene, it was at a bar called Happy's. But Avery's phone was brought there, and then they were both taken to Philadelphia."

"Whose phone was it?"

"Somebody named Eric Otero."

"Who is he?"

"I don't know; never heard of him. But I've got his address."

IT TURNS OUT THAT ERIC OTERO IS THE FRIEND OF VINCE PETRI'S WHO was smart enough to run away the night we confronted Petri.

Marcus and I are on the way to pay him a visit tonight. Marcus has spoken to him once since we met him the first time, and while he gave us some information about Petri, he's going to talk a lot more tonight.

We will not accept anything less.

We're going to his house in downtown Paterson. If he's not there, we'll look for him at Happy's, the bar he and Petri and the other lowlifes hang out in. But it's early, only eight thirty, so Otero might not have left for the bar yet.

Usually, when we're planning confrontations like this, Marcus takes a couple of days to learn the target's habits, so that we're not surprised by what we might run into. That didn't happen this time; we want to deal with Otero right away.

Marcus doesn't seem particularly worried by the lack of preparation, and if Marcus isn't worried, then neither am I.

Lights are on in Otero's house when we pull up. We don't know if he's married or lives with someone. But he could have an entire marine battalion as his roommates and it does not matter; we are going in.

We go up the steps and ring the doorbell. Marcus and I step to each side as we wait, just in case Otero decides to shoot through the door rather than talk to us. Marcus is holding a handgun, in case we in turn decide that the smart thing to do would be to shoot back.

But the door opens uneventfully, and Otero is standing there, eating an apple. "Oh, shit," he says, accurately capturing his feelings about this moment.

"Hello, Eric. Good to see you again," I say. "Are you going to invite us in?"

"No."

"You're quite a kidder, you know that?" I say as we walk in. Marcus pushes him backward as we enter, and Otero nearly loses his balance, but rights himself before falling.

"You guys got no right. This is my house. I can call the cops."

"Yes, you can. When you speak to them, you should tell them to send an ambulance as well. And maybe the coroner."

"Come on, what do you want? I didn't do anything."

Marcus has not said a word, but Otero does not take his eyes off him. He has seen Marcus in action, so Otero knows what he can do. Otero also saw me in action, but seems less intimidated by me. I feel slightly insulted by this.

"Tell us about the night that Vince Petri killed Danny Avery."

"I don't know nothing about it. I already told him that," Otero says, referring to Marcus.

"Actually, you do; we just need to jog your memory a bit. Do you remember driving to Philadelphia with Avery's phone? Does that ring a bell for you?"

"No . . . I don't know . . ."

"Eric, cop killers do not do well in custody at all. You know why? It's because they are in the custody of other cops. When you think about it, it's understandable why they would be pissed off."

"I didn't kill anybody."

I'm pretty sure he's telling the truth about that. Petri brought the phone to Otero that night at the bar. "Eric, it's decision time. You can tell us what happened, right here and now, or you can tell the cops about it in an hour. I can guarantee that you will never make a more important decision in your life."

He thinks about it for a few seconds and nods. "Okay. I'll tell you. But I did not kill no cop. I was not even there."

"We're waiting, Eric."

"That night I was at this bar where we hang out. I got there about eight thirty. Vince, he wasn't there, and then a little after nine he shows up. He's like all worked up, you know, like he was on something. But Vince didn't take no drugs, so it was crazy, you know?

"Anyway, he starts drinking; I mean, he must have had six shots in a row. That's not how he normally drank; usually he took things slow.

"I asked him what was going on, but he didn't answer that. He just told me that he had a job for me, and he'd pay me five hundred bucks, cash. I needed the money, but I didn't like the sound of it. I mean, if Vince is giving me five hundred bucks, the job had to be something bad, you know?

"But all he wanted was for me to go to Philadelphia and deliver a phone to somebody. He gave it to me in an envelope;

the envelope was open, so I could see what was inside. He said that I just had to leave it in a certain mailbox and call him when it was done. He said to make sure that nobody saw me do it. So that's what I did."

"Did you see anyone at the house where the mailbox was?"

"No, but there were some lights on. I didn't know Vince had killed anyone, I swear it. I didn't put it together until the next day, when I read about it. I talked to Vince, and he told me he didn't kill the cop, that the phone had nothing to do with that."

"And you believed him?"

Otero shakes his head and says softly, "No."

There's nothing else to be learned from Otero. I will turn all of the information over to Pete, who will take it to the prosecutor, and it will be determined whether any charges should be filed against Otero. I believe that Otero did not participate in the murder, but I wouldn't bet actual money on it.

If Otero tells the cops what he told us, then the Danny Avery murder case can probably be closed. Combined with the other information we've accumulated, Otero's saying that Petri had Avery's phone should be enough to declare the case solved, that Vince Petri murdered Danny Avery.

All in all, a decent night's work.

"YOU NEED TO GET YOUR ASS DOWN HERE," SPECIAL AGENT OLIVER Baron says when I answer the phone.

"Shirley? Is that you? I told you never to call me here."

"Don't be a wiseass. Get down here now."

I ask Baron what it's about, but he tells me we'll talk when I get there. He doesn't sound happy or patient, so I tell him I'm on my way. Which I am.

There's no sense wondering what he wants; I'm going to know soon enough. But if I had to guess, I'm thinking it's about Ian Solis, and it's not good.

I'm ushered into Baron's office as soon as I arrive. That alone breaks FBI unwritten rule number 4,338 . . . always keep visitors waiting, no matter what.

There is no small talk. "I'm going to tell you something. If you speak to anyone about it, I will send twenty federal agents to dismember you and feed you to sharks."

Something about what he just said triggers something in my mind, and even though I can't think of what it is, I know it's not fear. Baron is the only person in this room who is afraid.

"Understood."

"We have heard from Ian Solis, and we have two weeks. Actually twelve days now."

"Blackmail?"

"Yes."

"He's going to do something terrible, and you have no way of stopping it?"

"Yes."

"So you'll have to pay him?"

"No comment."

"Any guarantee that if you pay him, he'll then back off?"

"No comment."

"You want to tell me what it is he's threatening?"

"No. Now it's your turn. Tell me everything you've learned that could help us."

"I'll tell you everything I've learned, but I'm afraid it's not going to help you."

So I tell him everything . . . all about Arthur Rucker, Frank Gilmore, Jacob Richardson, Wilson Dozier, Sonny Davenport . . . I lay it all out, but I don't have a word to say about Ian Solis.

"I wouldn't even know Solis's name if Jimmy Dietrich hadn't printed out those newspaper articles and you hadn't told me the rest."

"Shit."

"My sentiments exactly. But if there's any advice I could give, it's to get ahold of Arthur Rucker and shake him down. Search every crevice of his office and his house; this whole thing revolves around him."

Baron stares at me. "If anything related to this situation comes up, no matter how trivial it might seem, I want to be the first call you make. Understand?"

"Totally."

I feel for Baron and would do anything I could to help. But Solis has barely been involved in what we're doing; I don't know if he has any role to play in it or not.

It's not like I can take out the Ian Solis file, read through it, and solve the case. That's especially true since I don't even have an Ian Solis file. All I have are the two media articles that Jimmy Dietrich printed out.

It's just one of the many questions that Jimmy could answer if he were here.

But he's not.

So it is up to us to answer them.

I HEAD TO LAURIE'S FROM MY MEETING IN NEWARK WITH AGENT BARON.

My first decision is whether to tell Laurie about the situation with Ian Solis. Baron threatened me with dismemberment and becoming shark food if I spoke to anyone, but I did not promise that I wouldn't. All I said was that I "understood."

I quite literally trust Laurie with my life, and she has demonstrated she is completely worthy of that trust. So I decide to share it with Laurie because she is my partner on this case, and she will be trying to stop Solis as much as I will. In my view this information is on a need-to-know basis, and for Laurie to be an effective investigator, she needs to know it.

So when I get there, I tell her about the meeting. The other advantage in sharing it with her is that this way I don't have to be the only person who is so frustrated that my head is going to explode.

"We need to keep doing what we're doing," she says. "That's the only possible way for us to impact this situation. If it turns out Solis is a part of it, then maybe we can bring him down."

She's right. But it's hard for us to keep doing what we're doing if we don't know what we're doing.

"Did Baron say whether they were going to pick up Rucker for questioning?"

"He didn't say, but my guess is he will. He's a pro and not prone to making rash acts that could become mistakes, but I sensed desperation, so I don't think there is anything they won't try. What Solis is threatening to do must be really bad."

"So what do we focus on?"

"I would say both Jacob Richardson and Arthur Rucker. If we can figure out who Richardson really was, that could open some doors. And I say Rucker because everything seems to begin and end with him."

"Okay," Laurie says. "I'm going to ask Sam to dig deeper. Maybe he can trace Richardson's movements in the last few months through his phone, and that could tell us something."

I nod. "And I'm going back through the file Viola sent me on Rucker and the Wingate murder of his partner, Wilson Dozier. I've read through it once, but will do it again, and there are some tapes for me to look at. Maybe he made a mistake that the Philly cops didn't pick up on."

I head home. Dani is still in Vegas, and Simon has been cooped up for a while; so I take him for a long walk. It gives me time to think about the case and hopefully see it from a fresh perspective.

It doesn't quite work out that way. I do a lot of thinking, but come up with the same old perspectives that haven't gotten us anywhere.

When I get back, I feed Simon and make myself one of the

few dishes I don't screw up, raisin bran and milk, with a cut-up banana in it. I definitely show chef potential.

Stuffed from that delicious dinner, I settle in to read about Arthur Rucker. It's nothing I haven't read before, and I don't get any more out of it this time than I did before.

But there is one new addition that I hadn't seen before. At my request, Lieutenant Viola had made copies of video recordings and sent them on to me. They're in some kind of thing that I just plug into the side of my computer, and video appears!

What a world.

It starts with recordings of the three interrogation sessions that Philadelphia PD conducted with Arthur Rucker. The sessions seem similar to his with me; Rucker came with his attorney each time and was basically unruffled and in control.

Each session lasts more than an hour, and I find myself fast-forwarding through it because I am learning nothing at all new. It's not surprising; if Rucker had said anything incriminating or revealing, then the Philly cops would have picked up on it.

At the end is the video taken by the security cameras when Wingate forced Wilson Dozier onto the boat. It's a little dark, though there is enough moonlight to see, and there seems to be one light on a pole there as well.

As Viola had described, Wingate has a gun in Dozier's back as he pushes him onto the boat. I can't see Wingate's face very well, but Dozier seems agitated and resistant. But he can do nothing; he knows he is about to become shark food.

Shark food.

Viola had used that term, and Baron had said if I revealed what he said, he would dismember me and feed my body to sharks.

The next video shows the boat returning and only Wingate getting off. This time he is facing the camera, and I can see him clearly. It's the first time I've seen Wingate since he was lying dead in my backyard.

There's only one problem.

The person in the video is not Wingate.

Or maybe the person who tried to kill me was not Wingate.

But one of those things has to be true because the person on the boat and the one I killed in my backyard are not the same person.

And suddenly I know why.

I DON'T THINK LAURIE IS COMPLETELY CONVINCED BY WHAT I AM SAYING.

I know that because she has just said, "I'm not completely convinced by what you're saying."

"I saw his face that night very clearly while he was lying there."

"He was dead. People look different when they're dead. And that video is not that clear."

"They don't look that different. And it was clear enough for the Philly cops to put out a warrant for his arrest."

"Okay. I have to admit it's an interesting theory. And we'll know soon enough."

She's right. Our conversation won't solve anything, but the good news is it won't have to. I've sent a copy of a coroner's photograph of the guy I killed, the guy DNA identified as Joey Wingate, to Lieutenant Viola in Philadelphia. We're just waiting for her to get in this morning, look at it, and call us.

A half hour later, a long half hour later, the call comes in. "What the hell is going on?"

"You looked at the photograph?"

"I did. That is not Joey Wingate. Which brings me back to my original question. . . . What the hell is going on?"

"It's a very long story."

"I have time."

"I don't, but I promise to fill you in."

"Should I put the warrant for Wingate back in the system? Didn't the damn DNA match?"

"Just hold off for a while; don't do anything. I promise I'll clear the whole thing up."

She keeps pressing me, but I'm not about to tell her any more. This is another example of something being on a need-to-know basis, and Lieutenant Viola is currently out of the loop.

Laurie and I start to plan our next steps, and we bring Andy into the conversation. We can go a number of ways, and we are kicking them around when Sam calls.

"I thought you'd want to know this. I've been tracing the movements of Arthur Rucker's phone, and it left Philadelphia this morning."

"Where did it go?"

"I'm not positive, because it seems to be in a moving car, and it's still going. But the direction it's headed so far, my guess is the Demarest Hotel."

"Sam, this is very important . . . keep tracking it and let me know where it ends up."

"Will do."

I'm not at all surprised by Sam's news; it fits my theory perfectly. I go on Laurie's computer and call up the website for the Demarest, and it shows that they've just begun the two weeks during which the hotel will be closed to guests for renovations.

Rucker had said that is his favorite time to be there, but I suspect this time things are a bit different from his past visits.

This development, if it's confirmed by Sam when the phone
is no longer in motion, crystallizes what our next step must be.

I have to go to the Demarest Hotel.

But this time I won't be ordering the soufflé.

SAM HAS CONFIRMED THAT RUCKER, OR AT LEAST HIS PHONE, IS AT THE Demarest.

My first call this morning is to Steven Barkley, the owner-manager of the hotel.

He doesn't sound thrilled to hear from me, but I'm not offended. "I really don't have any more information for you. I've tried."

"I understand; that's not why I'm calling. I want to visit your hotel tomorrow."

"We're closed for the next two weeks. But after that, I would be happy to make a reservation for you myself."

"I don't want to come as a guest. I'm coming to talk to Arthur Rucker."

He's quiet for a few moments, unsure how to respond. "What makes you think Mr. Rucker is here?"

"He told me that he likes going when the hotel is empty;

that way he doesn't have to deal with your peasant guests in the lobby."

"That doesn't mean—"

"I know he's there, Mr. Barkley. I'm a detective; I detected it. I understand you're trying to protect your guests, but I'm not going to injure or attack him. We're just going to have a talk."

"Will you be bringing official law enforcement personnel with you?"

"That's not my current plan."

"I really don't think this is appropriate. Mr. Rucker seems to value his privacy, and—"

"I'm not asking your permission. I'm just giving you a heads-up that I'm coming. If you try and stop me, then I can assure you the hotel will suddenly be swarming with 'official law enforcement personnel.'"

He is silent for a few moments, then seems to concede. "When will you be arriving?"

"Sometime tomorrow, probably early afternoon."

"You know I guard the privacy of our guests and apartment owners, so I have to ask that you come well after lunch. Mr. Rucker is having people over for a luncheon tomorrow. He's asked that I have the kitchen open."

"What time is that lunch?"

"One o'clock. It's scheduled for two hours. Please don't intrude on it."

"I wouldn't mind seeing who his lunch guests are."

"Detective Douglas—"

"Okay, after lunch. I'll be there at three. I am nothing if not reasonable."

"Mr. Rucker is a prominent businessman. What is it you think he has done wrong?"

"How does multiple murders sound?"

"Oh . . . this is a nightmare."

"It's no walk in the park, that's for sure."

"Please do not discuss with Mr. Rucker the fact that I was apprised of these arrangements."

"My lips are sealed. See you tomorrow."

I GOT ABOUT FOUR HOURS SLEEP LAST NIGHT. I WAS AT LAURIE'S UNTIL past midnight going over strategy with her, Andy, and Marcus.

Then, when I got home, I couldn't get to sleep for a while as I was running the various scenarios through my mind. I would say about half of the scenarios worked out well, which is not as high a percentage as I would usually hope for.

I left for the Demarest at about 9:00 A.M., which was two hours ago. I'm not nervous, which does not surprise me. Lack of nerves is sort of a gift I've somehow been given. So I have to force myself to be cautious, something normal people come to naturally because of their nervousness.

I once read about someone who never felt physical pain, no matter what. While that would seem like a good thing, it was actually the opposite. Pain is the way the body warns us that something is wrong; not to experience it means not knowing about the problem, and thus not treating it.

Nervousness and anxiety are triggers to get us to be careful; so I have to compensate for my lack of those things by logically forcing myself to act with caution. I'm not saying I'm never nervous; I can get anxious in some social situations. But never from danger; I don't know why, but that's the way I am wired.

I'm about an hour from the Demarest when my phone rings. I see by the caller ID that it's from the US government, and for a moment I consider not answering it, but I quickly reject that idea.

"Hello."

"It's Agent Baron. Your friend is missing."

"Which friend might that be?"

"Arthur Rucker. We went to pick him up for questioning, and he was nowhere to be found. His wife said he never came home last night and she has no idea where he is."

"And you're calling me why?"

"To see if you know where he is."

I'm torn here; I want to get to Rucker before Baron does. If he shows up with the cavalry at the Demarest, it could blow everything up.

The chance I am taking is immense. If I screw this up, it will literally be a disaster of unprecedented dimensions. But I think there's a better chance for success this way, so I am following my gut.

"Okay, Baron, I'm going to be straight with you. I'm in the middle of something that I think is going to solve both of our problems. If I'm wrong, it won't make matters worse; you can still do what you're going to do."

"What the hell are you talking about?"

"You'll find out. For the time being, be prepared to travel. Helicopters would be a good idea. My partner Laurie Collins will call you within the next two hours and tell you what to do."

He is furious. *"This is not how it's done, Douglas! You are screwing with the wrong people!"*

"It's how it's being done today, Baron. I'm on your side; you're going to have to trust me."

"Why should I trust you?"

"Because you have no choice."

Baron could trace my cell phone to follow my movements, but he would not know whether I am going anywhere significant to him. He would also not want to accidentally blunder into anything and make matters worse. So all he can do is wait.

I hang up and can picture his head exploding in his office. If this does not work out, I am in deep shit.

WHEN I GET TO THE BURGER KING ABOUT A HALF HOUR FROM THE Demarest, I stop for lunch.

I haven't had anything to eat all day, and I'm starved. I'm also superstitious; I stopped here the last time I drove to the hotel, and I didn't get killed the entire day. Hopefully that happens again.

I wish I had Simon with me; I just feel more comfortable in these situations when he is around. But it's not set up for him to have a role, and he could be in danger if he were here. But he'll be pissed when he finds out what he missed.

Eventually I get to the hotel, once again driving past the service road leading to the back of the place and going straight to the front. Because it's closed for renovations, no valet or bellman is there to greet me with "Welcome to the Demarest, sir."

There is also no sign of renovations being done, no workers and no trucks or equipment. Not a big surprise, but noteworthy.

I also do not see any cars, owned either by Arthur Rucker or his alleged lunch guests.

I go up the steps and enter the hotel. If there is a moment of extreme danger, this is it. I'm wearing a bulletproof vest under my jacket, but it obviously does not cover my head. I'm alert for any sound or sudden movement, but there is none; the place seems deserted.

"Welcome, Detective." Steven Barkley, smiling and at ease, enters from the other side of the lobby. "You're early. Our agreement was three o'clock."

"The GPS took me on a faster route. Nice place you have here."

"Thank you."

"Where's Rucker?"

"I believe he is upstairs in his apartment, but I just got here a short time ago myself, so I can't be sure."

"What happened to his luncheon?"

"Fortunately, he canceled it this morning. I'll take you up to Mr. Rucker's apartment, and you can knock on the door. That's the best I can do."

"I can find it on my own."

"I'm sure you can, but the elevator won't work without my key."

We walk to the elevator that leads up to the seventh and eighth floors. As I turn the corner, I see that another man is standing there, waiting for us. I've never before seen him. He is large, maybe six foot three and at least 240, without any noticeable fat.

Of course, at the moment I'm not searching his body for fat; my eyes are focused on the gun he is pointing at me. My own gun is in my pocket; Wyatt Earp couldn't draw it fast enough if he were in my position.

"Detective Douglas, meet Curtis," Barkley says. "He's heard a great deal about you."

"Hey, Curtis, what's happening?"

Curtis doesn't respond, but Barkley quickly frisks me and takes my gun from my pocket.

"Let's all get on the elevator, shall we?" Barkley says.

I don't move; I just say, "You're calling the shots, Mr. Dozier."

"You figured out that I'm Wilson Dozier? Very impressive."

"People told me Dozier was shark food, but I knew better. I knew Dozier was the slimy, weasel asshole who runs the Demarest Hotel."

"You won't be quite so confident very soon," Barkley, now Dozier, says. "The elevator?"

I still stand there; the longer this takes the better. "You're taking me up to Rucker's apartment because you want it to look like he killed me. And maybe I killed him in the same gunfight."

Curtis raises the gun a bit farther. "Move. Now."

"Wow," I say. "He speaks. One-syllable words, but even so . . . I would have thought all he could do was drool."

I move to the elevator and finally get on, followed by Curtis and Barkley. Barkley waves his key at the control pad, and we're on the way up. The elevator is as slow as I remember it, which in this case is a good thing.

This is clearly not Curtis's first time handling a gun; he keeps his distance from me and never wavers on how he is pointing it. There is no way I can take it away from him, and I'm not planning to try.

Barkley holds my gun, but he is less of a threat. He's not even pointing it; he obviously has confidence in his colleague.

If Curtis were not on this elevator with us, I would have disarmed Barkley before we even got past the third floor. He would be unconscious around the time we passed six.

We finally get to eight, and the door opens. Curtis makes a motion with the gun to signal me to go first, and I do. Curtis follows me, but as he walks off the elevator, he is smashed in the head by a tree trunk that seems to fall from the sky. The tree trunk is actually an arm, attached to Marcus's shoulder.

Dozier reacts to what has happened with surprise, which slows down his reaction time. We're talking fractions of seconds, but that's time for me to turn and knock the gun out of his hand. Then I punch him as hard as I can in the side of the head, between the left temple and left eye socket.

The punch lands solid, and even though it hurts my hand, it feels great to land it. He goes straight down, landing half in the hallway and half in the elevator, preventing the door from closing. It keeps trying to, smacking into Barkley's prone body and then backing off, then smacking into it again.

It's actually pretty funny.

"Thanks, Marcus."

He doesn't say anything, just bends over and handcuffs Dozier's hands behind his back. Then he does the same to Curtis, who looks like he won't wake up until the turn of the next century.

We don't want either of them regaining consciousness and causing us any problems. They're both currently facedown, so the handcuffing is easy.

I dial Laurie on my cell phone, and when she answers, I say, "You can call Baron."

"Got it." She hangs up.

Baron and his people will be here soon, and if we don't succeed, then they can try their way. But it's our turn first.

Now comes the hard part.

THERE ARE THREE APARTMENTS ON THIS FLOOR BESIDES THE UNOCCU-
pied one that I toured the last time I was here.

I'm pretty sure that Rucker is in one of them, but that's not the one I'm interested in, at least right now. I'm looking for Ian Solis.

The last time I was here, the hotel manager previously known as Barkley told me that only one of the apartments at the time was currently occupied. I'm betting that is Solis's home base, and Solis must be the guy I saw getting off the elevator that day. Barkley referred to him as Walters.

A room service tray was on the floor outside one of the apartments that day, which makes me fairly certain that is Solis's. If I'm wrong, then I'll move on to the next one . . . no harm, no foul. But I don't think I'm wrong.

The door is locked. So with my gun in my right hand, I knock on the door with my left, then step to the side.

After about five seconds, the door slowly opens. I enter cautiously, gun drawn, but I don't see anyone. Wherever Solis is, he probably has the door hooked up to open when he presses a button. If he has the technological expertise to bring Homeland Security to its knees, rigging a door must be a piece of cake.

The door just as quickly closes behind me. I still don't see Solis or anyone else. I'm not feeling in control here.

"Come back to my office," a voice I assume is Solis's calls out.

I follow the sound to what Barkley had described as the den in the unoccupied apartment. I look in and see a desk with at least four computers on it, with other monitors on walls nearby. This is obviously Solis's base of operations; it looks like the deck of the starship *Enterprise*.

As I walk in, I feel a gun placed in my back.

"Now drop the gun."

I do so, and he tells me to walk farther into the room, which I do as well. "Sit down over there."

I take the seat he's indicating.

He walks around behind his desk, keeping his gun trained on me. He's now in front of his computer consoles. We see each other through the space between two of the computers. It's also the space through which he points the gun at me.

"I hooked up a speaker in here, so that's where you thought my voice was coming from, and you followed it. I was led to believe that you were better than that.

"I told Dozier not to bring you here today. But I couldn't tell him why because he had no idea what I was doing. Do you believe that? I've been working with him all this time, and he had no idea. He thought what we were doing was an end in itself."

"He's not quite as big an asshole as you are. Very few people are."

Solis smiles. "Tough guy, huh? You know what I just

realized? You're the only person I can talk to about this. I can't trust anybody else; I learned that the hard way. But you won't be around to tell anybody, so I can tell you anything."

"I'm glad I can be here for you."

He ignores that. "This new development is forcing me to change the plan, but I'm flexible. I'm going to bring down the Eastern Interconnection Grid in a few minutes. You probably don't even know what it is, so you have no idea of the chaos that will create.

"Within thirty-six hours, it will turn half of the United States into a third-world country, and then it will get far worse. No heat, no light, no gas, no water, no food supply chain . . . and then the looting and violence will start. But don't worry, I've prepared for it myself." He laughs. "And you won't be affected by it at all."

"You don't think they'll catch you?"

He laughs. "How can they catch someone who doesn't exist?"

"There's one thing I should point out. No big deal, but worth mentioning. My partner came up through the back entrance and is over there, behind you to your left, holding a gun on you. Whenever she wants, she can blow your pathetic head off."

He shakes his head, unworried. He keeps his eyes and gun trained on me. "Once again you disappoint me. I really thought you were better than that."

"You should put down the gun; it's your only chance to survive. I'm only telling you this because I feel like we've become buddies, even though you are . . . you know . . . a piece of raw sewage."

He frowns; I don't think he believes me.

"Good-bye, Detective Douglas."

He raises the gun slightly to point it at my head; I'm not sure he knows about the bulletproof vest.

But it doesn't matter. The partner that he didn't believe was holding a gun on him shoots him in the head, specifically behind the left temple.

He falls into the area between the computers as Laurie walks toward him to confirm that another shot won't be necessary. It won't.

I come around to the other side of the desk to join her. "Nice shot."

"Thanks, but it would have been better to keep him alive."

"I know, but there was nothing you could do. You called Agent Baron?"

"I did. He should get here in about forty-five minutes. I told him to bring tech people with him."

"What was his attitude?"

"I would describe it as extremely annoyed. He said something about putting you behind bars for the rest of your life."

"That seems ungrateful."

I look at the amazing array of computers on Solis's desk, and the rest of the room. "I could use a setup like this."

"For sending emails?"

"I do more than send emails on computers. I also play solitaire and check scores on ESPN."

MARCUS LIFTS UP DOZIER, WHO IS ABLE TO STAND ON HIS OWN.

Maybe I don't hit as hard as I think. I certainly don't hit as hard as Marcus because Curtis remains in never-never land. Marcus puts both of them on the elevator to take them downstairs.

I'm pretty sure that Arthur Rucker is in one of the other apartments; I hope he's alive. So I grab Dozier's master key and open the door to the apartment next to Solis's.

I look around the apartment, and sure enough, there is Arthur Rucker, in the bedroom. He's sitting in a chair, bound and gagged, but very much among the living.

I put my gun down on the dresser, so he won't think I'm here to hurt him. As I walk toward him, I say, "Rucker, I'm afraid I owe you an apology. I accused you of some bad things. On the other hand, I've just saved your life. Can we call it even?"

I take the gag off and he says, "We're even."

We go downstairs to wait for Agent Baron and his people. They arrive after about thirty minutes, on three helicopters. It's an impressive display; they land in an open area near the front of the hotel. Unfortunately, there are no bellmen to greet them, and no valet people to give them a ticket and park the choppers.

Baron is the first person off, and he comes straight toward us. "What's the situation?" All the other agents, and there must be twenty of them, stand there waiting for him to tell them what to do.

"Solis is upstairs on the eighth floor."

"Is he armed?"

"Yes, but he's also dead."

"You're sure about that?"

"Quite positive. Solis's computer setup is also up there . . . hopefully you brought some people that can work it."

He sees Arthur Rucker sitting on the steps, still looking a bit dazed by what he's gone through. "That's Rucker. Why isn't he cuffed?"

"Because it turns out he's not a crook after all. My bad."

Then Baron notices Dozier, and that his face is badly bruised and he is in handcuffs. "Who is he?"

"That's actually a more complicated question than you might think, and at the moment not important. I'll explain it all later."

"What about him?" Baron points to the unconscious Curtis.

"That's Curtis, last name currently unknown. He was apparently in charge of violence for the operation."

"What happened to him?"

"Marcus Clark. Come on, I'll take you upstairs."

I lead Baron and most of the other agents to the elevator. Five of them stay behind in what must be some kind of tactical maneuver, in case more adversaries show up.

"Are there stairs?" Baron asks.

"Over there." Five of the agents head for the stairs; I guess Baron doesn't want the entire "attack team" in one vulnerable elevator.

We get on, and I wave Barkley's master key against the elevator control panel.

Baron has drawn his gun, as have the other agents.

"Nobody is going to shoot at you. You can trust me on that."

Apparently I'm not all that trustworthy because they don't put their guns away. Baron is the first one out of the elevator, and we all follow. I take them into Solis's apartment.

Baron quickly moves to the computers and Solis's dead body, wedged between them. "Who is that?"

"Ian Solis."

He turns Solis's bloody head to get a better look, then gets angry. "What is going on here? That is not Solis."

"Remember downstairs when I told you things were complicated?"

"YOU SHOULD THINK OF IT AS A BIZARRO WITNESS PROTECTION PRO-gram," I say, after Baron takes me into another room to talk.

Baron looks confused, and I don't blame him. "I don't know what that means."

"It's as if they created a protection program for bad guys. In most cases, they were people on the run or otherwise looking to escape their lives. They had big money, either earned or more often stolen, and they were willing to pay the price."

"Price for what?"

"For new lives; like you do with witnesses, but way more sophisticated. They had a surgeon who performed radical plastic surgery on them; so radical that I found out that even their wives would not recognize them.

"It was done on premises here; they have a medical setup on the seventh floor. I haven't been in there, but I'd bet there's a fully equipped operating room. After the surgery, the clients spent their recovery and healing time in an apartment on this floor, where no one would ever look for them.

"But Solis was the key. He was a genius online, as you already know. He created new identities for each client, an actual new life, with a full background that could withstand anything but the most intense scrutiny.

"So by the time the clients left Camp Demarest, they were ready to enter society, pretty much anywhere they wanted. They had a new identity, a new face, and plenty of money."

"That's why I didn't recognize Solis," Baron says, finally understanding.

I nod. "Right. After he got the blackmail money or destroyed the grid, which he was definitely planning to do, by the way, he would have gone free. You never could have found him because he no longer existed as Ian Solis."

Baron takes a few moments to digest all of this and finally says, "If I were you, I would block out at least a month on my schedule for a debriefing."

"I don't think so, but I will tell you everything I know. Why don't we meet in Andy's office . . . the one above the fruit stand."

"You realize this could have blown up in your face, and if it did, you'd be in handcuffs now."

He's right, but I don't want to concede it. "Not really. If I got killed, Laurie would still have told you where Solis was, which was information you would not have had before. You could have then gone after him in whatever way you wanted."

"You took a stupid risk."

"I've got to tell you, Agent Baron, I'm not feeling a lot of gratitude. Very disappointing."

Baron pauses. "You did good. Thanks." For him that qualifies as effusive, gushing praise.

He has more questions for me, and not surprisingly he is far more interested in all things Solis-related than the original conspiracy. That will gradually change when he realizes that quite a few people that have gone through the new-identification program might be on the FBI's most wanted list.

Laurie speaks for the first time. "You should know that this entire, very successful operation was done under the supervision of Captain Pete Stanton of the Paterson Police Department."

"Thanks for sharing that," Baron says with some disdain.

"No problem. And that needs to make its way into the media, or we will schedule our own press conference."

Baron just nods; I think he gets the message.

Two more helicopters land with still more people, after which two cars and two vans pull up as well. The Demarest has not had this many visitors in a long time.

I explain Dozier's role in the situation, so that he can be taken into custody along with Curtis, who has finally regained semiconsciousness. I also tell Baron to find and arrest Dr. Powers; without him none of this would have been possible.

Since there is no reason to detain Rucker, he makes some phone calls and apparently arranges his exit from the scene.

I'd love to get a ride back in one of the helicopters, but I want to get out of here as well. I suspect Baron and the agents will be dealing with this scene for a long time. Besides, we have two cars, mine and the one Laurie and Marcus came in.

So we're out of here.

SINCE PETE SUPERVISED THE ENTIRE OPERATION, LAURIE AND I THOUGHT
we should stop by and tell him what he supervised.

Marcus didn't want to be here, but we brought Simon along
in case we need protection.

Pete starts the meeting by telling us that he just got word
from the commissioner that he is to appear at a Homeland Security press conference at 3:00 P.M. "You guys want to tell me
what this is about?"

We start by telling him all that happened at the Demarest
Hotel yesterday, since we're sure that will be the main subject
of the press conference. Homeland Security is going to want to
send a message to people who would like to be the next Ian Solis
that things will not work out so well for them if they try it.

Not surprisingly, Pete has a truckload of questions for us,
but he starts with the key one: "So can we close the cases you
were hired to investigate?"

"Mostly," I say. "We know for sure that Vince Petri killed Danny Avery, and that it was ordered by Dozier. I suspect you're going to have to fight the Feds for custody of Dozier and Curtis, and I doubt you'll win. I can't imagine them giving them up; their crimes are interstate."

Pete nods. "What about Susan Avery and Jimmy Dietrich?"

"Definitely ordered by Dozier. Probably carried out by Joey Wingate, or maybe Curtis, but no way to know for sure. Maybe Dozier or Curtis will talk to avoid the death penalty, but absent that we'll never know."

"Good enough to close the cases; nice job," Pete says. "Where did Rucker fit into all of this?"

"He didn't," I say. "They were setting him up in case things went wrong. They staged Dozier's death on the water; because he was 'shark food,' his body was never found. That made Rucker look suspect. Then they killed Jimmy and Susan on a boat, to make the crimes seem similar. And then they brought Danny Avery's phone to Rucker's house, in case the GPS was checked. They didn't miss a trick. Dozier even talked Rucker into buying an apartment at the Demarest, so if things blew up there, everyone and everything would point to him."

Laurie adds, "They used Wingate to come after Corey at his house that night because Wingate was tied to Rucker. Wingate was in the program and got a new identity and a new face. We think he didn't pay money to get in, but promised to do jobs for them as they needed it."

"How did they find candidates that were going on the run?"

Laurie says, "Baron thinks it's done on the dark web. I'm sure the Feds will dig into that."

"So Frank Gilmore, the guy Avery killed in the domestic violence thing . . . he was not really Frank Gilmore?"

"No," I say. "We don't know who he was. And Jacob

Richardson was not Jacob Richardson; he was either Roger Linder or someone we don't know about yet. DNA will determine that. But their previous identities ceased to exist; in almost every sense of the word they were new people. They were on the run, but had no reason to have to hide."

Laurie adds, "Danny Avery must have been out to prove that Gilmore was not what he seemed, this benevolent philanthropist. In the process, he must have stumbled onto this. He kept pulling on the thread, which led him to George Hafner and Marcella's that night."

I nod. "And Hafner told a friend he would disappear one day. He didn't mean he'd get killed; he was expecting to be part of the new identity program. They used him and then killed him."

"So now you expect me to go to this press conference and claim credit for all this?" Pete asks.

"If you don't, the Feds will, and all they did was go on a helicopter ride," I say. "We're part of your department; you're our leader. You pay us to do your bidding. We worship the ground you walk on."

"Speaking of paying you, I saw your expense report. Six hundred goddamn dollars a night for a hotel room?"

"It's his fault." I point at Simon. "He heard they had great biscuits."

"SO HOW DID YOU FIGURE IT OUT?" DANI ASKS. SHE'S JUST BACK FROM Vegas, and we haven't yet talked in depth about the resolution of the case.

"I'm never really sure about that. When I'm lucky, something happens or is said and all the pieces just click into place. In this case I should have known it earlier."

"What is it that happened?"

"Joey Wingate. The DNA could not have been wrong, so when his appearance was so different, there had to be a reason why. Changing appearance, along with Richardson changing his identity, was the ideal situation for people on the run hoping not to be found. And everybody seemed to have the money to make it happen."

"And then there was the surgeon."

"Right. All of a sudden his role became clear. And once I had this theory, then Solis's place in it was obvious. He was able to create fake people in cyberspace. And the fact that Dozier's body was never found, that he was 'shark food,' was another piece that suddenly made sense.

"And then you helped as well."

"How?"

"You said you were going to check in to the hotel in Vegas under a fake name to protect yourself. I know you were kidding, but that is a way to escape detection. These people used fake names, but they faked everything. They became different people."

"So this is another triumph for me?"

"Definitely."

She smiles. "So what's our next case?"